BEYOND
+HE
WALL

EDITED BY JAMES LOWDER

BEYOND

THE

WALL

• • •

EXPLORING
GEORGE R.R. MARTIN'S
A SONG OF ICE AND FIRE
FROM *A Game Of Thrones* TO *A Dance with Dragons*

AN IMPRINT OF BENBELLA BOOKS, INC.| DALLAS, TEXAS

Beyond the Wall: Exploring George R.R. Martin's A Song of Ice and Fire, From A Game of Thrones to A Dance with Dragons © 2012 by James Lowder

BenBella Books, Inc.
10300 N. Central Expressway, Suite 400
Dallas, TX 75231
www.benbellabooks.com
Send feedback to feedback@benbellabooks.com

Printed in the United States of America
10 9 8 7 6 5 4 3 2

Library of Congress Cataloging-in-Publication Data is available for this title.
978-1-936661-74-9

Copyediting by Margaret Wickham
Proofreading by Chris Gage and Michael Fedison
Cover design by Faceout Studio
Text design and composition by Neuwirth & Associates, Inc.
Printed by Berryville Graphics

Distributed by Perseus Distribution
(www.perseusdistribution.com)
To place orders through Perseus Distribution:
Tel: 800-343-4499
Fax: 800-351-5073
E-mail: orderentry@perseusbooks.com

Significant discounts for bulk sales are available. Please contact Glenn Yeffeth at glenn@benbellabooks.com or (214) 750-3628.

CONTENTS

FOREWORD

Stories for the Nights to Come

R.A. SALVATORE

WHY FANTASY?

Why write it? To entertain? To enlighten? To cut new alley-ways of allegory? To chase spirituality with magic?

It pains me when I hear Margaret Atwood claim that she's not a fantasy author, as if that label somehow diminishes the quality of her work, just as it pained me three decades ago when my favorite literature professor discovered that I was reading Tolkien's Lord of the Rings in my free time. How his face turned red with anger! He had been pushing me toward his beloved Brandeis, to follow in his literary training, and bristled at the notion that I was wasting my intellect with such drivel.

He is long retired, but Tolkien certainly isn't. The twilight fancies resound about us, in books, movies, and television. They dominate the nascent art form of video games.

But even today, the pushback remains, as professors teaching Gilgamesh and Beowulf, Homer and Dante, wonder the worth instead of the irony. So it follows: when we see specific works of fantasy fiction, such as George R.R. Martin's A Song of Ice and Fire series, threatening to break into the halls of respectability, there is an undercurrent of commentary seeking to discredit the notion that said praiseworthy works could actually be, well, fantasy. Whether it's the author's own statements, as with Ms. Atwood and Terry Goodkind, or the marketing angle attached to the books—Chris Paolini is a "child prodigy writing young adult stories"; Philip Pullman is writing religious (or antireligious) allegory; J.K. Rowling is carrying on the fine British tradition of prep-school tales—the notion that these wonderful works sit well under the label of fantasy is always downplayed. Could it be that they are fantasy and they are all of those other things the academics and the marketers say, as well? Of course, to all, or they wouldn't succeed.

Or could it be that they are none of those things, and the labels themselves cut too fine a pie slice to be worth the taste? Is there really a corner to be turned here? Can the brilliance of *The Handmaid's Tale* be diminished by a label attached to it? If that is the case, then we truly have found superficiality, but not in the work.

Peter Jackson accepted the slings and arrows of Hollywood royalty with his loving treatment of The Lord of the Rings as a serious and fantastical work. Millions of fans understood and appreciated his accomplishment, if the Academy did not, or did so only grudgingly. I hope my favorite college professor saw the films, and perhaps, if he did, the experience helped him to open his eyes, to understand, as Peter S. Beagle put it in the forward to the 1973 Ballantine edition of Tolkien's epic, that what Tolkien actually did was "to tap our most common nightmares, daydreams and twilight fancies, but he never invented them either: he found them a place to live, a green alternative to each day's madness here in a poisoned world."

Jackson's films have helped to reveal the absurdity of the label as condemnation. But if not Jackson, then certainly George Martin has done so, and hopefully for good.

I had the pleasure of sitting on a panel with George a few years ago; it felt more like we were sitting around a campfire on a dark winter's night, whispering of adventure. Listening to George recount the stories of a childhood spent reading is listening to a love letter to speculative fiction. There's no getting around it: George Martin writes fantasy—unabashedly, proudly, lovingly.

He also writes brilliant characters: heroes to cheer, and too often to cry for; villains to hate, but more than that, to understand (and, perhaps, to view as the dark sides of our own natures); monsters to make you ponder that most basic and profound human fear, the one to which, alas, there is no answer. It's no secret and no accident why he's so successful. His characters are real to him, it matters not their race, and he writes them with such affection that they become real to the reader.

That's the thing about fantasy. Set aside the strange trappings, erase the swirl of magic and strike the fairy-tale castles, and you have elves and dwarves and evil orcs that the author has to make, in the end, human; if the readers cannot identify with the sensibilities of these characters as they react to the pressure of their surroundings, the book, like any book shelved under any label, will fail.

So why fantasy? For the same reasons as any other kind of storytelling. A writer writes to get people asking questions more than to give them answers, and the ultimate achievement of literature is to begin a conversation. To read the essays that follow is to recognize the depth and breadth of the conversation A Song of Ice and Fire has started.

George Martin has woven for us the tapestry of Westeros, filled with resonating characters who see the world through a different and sometimes magical prism. And still we empathize, we sympathize, we live with and live through these exotic beings. We see enough truth of the human condition in each of them to fall in love or to spit with hate. Classify it anyway you'd like; call it fantasy, or low fantasy, or high fantasy, or allegory. Feel free to assign the label of your choice.

I'm sure those labels won't bother George, however they're applied or defined. Because what he knows, what the essayists in this volume and his millions of fans certainly know, is that what he really writes are damned great books, for this night and all the nights to come.

◆ ◆ ◆

With more than four-dozen books to his credit and over 17 million copies sold in the US alone, **R.A. SALVATORE** has become one of the most important figures in modern epic fantasy. His first break came in 1987 when TSR, Inc., publisher of *Dungeons & Dragons*, offered him a contract for a book set in the Forgotten Realms shared-world setting. Bob's first published novel, *The Crystal Shard*, was released in February 1988 and climbed to number two on the Waldenbooks bestseller list. By 1990 his third book, *The Halfling's Gem*, had made the *New York Times* list. With a contract for three more books from TSR, and his first creator-owned novel and its sequel sold to Penguin, Bob realized that "it seemed like a good time to quit my day job." In addition to his novel writing, Salvatore is involved in game design, most notably the creation of a brand-new world for 38 Studios, which serves as the setting for the *Kingdoms of Amalur: Reckoning* RPG and will also form the foundation for their first MMORPG, currently code-named *Copernicus*. He is currently at work writing the next and final installment of the Neverwinter Trilogy, due out in August 2012.

INTRODUCTION

In Praise of Living History

JAMES LOWDER

IN AUGUST 1996, WHEN *A Game of Thrones* first hit store shelves, the speculative fiction cognoscenti thought they knew what they had before them. For more than two decades, George R.R. Martin had been producing consistently smart, finely crafted prose in the service of predictably unpredictable plots. Industry insiders, along with fans and scholars of genre fiction, had saluted these works with an impressive array of nominations and awards, stretching all the way back to the early 1970s. A new Martin release was something to anticipate, at least for those in the know, and the smart money was on the book garnering several major award nominations, if not the statues themselves.

The few thousand readers who picked up the first printing of *A Game of Thrones* cracked it open and nodded knowingly at the grim, character-focused tale. As with many of Martin's earlier works, history and the fantasy tradition—in particular, lesser-known weird fantasy authors such as Mervyn Peake and Jack Vance—inform the rich setting. Scrape the paint on the house sigils and beneath the gold lions and grey direwolves you'll glimpse the red rose of Lancaster and the white rose of York. Map out the treacherous rooftops of Winterfell as Bran Stark races across them in play and you can see where he might well bump into Steerpike as that arch-schemer makes his own trek across the vast and crumbling roofscape of Castle Gormenghast.

As expected, the cognoscenti nominated *A Game of Thrones* for a World Fantasy Award and a Nebula, while the Spanish Science Fiction Association handed it an Ignotus for best foreign novel and the readers of the industry magazine *Locus* named it the year's best fantasy novel. An impressive debut for a new series, but nothing that suggested the books would get much traction with audiences beyond the science fiction convention circuit. Reviewers in more mainstream markets, such as the *Washington Post*, echoed that sentiment when they declared the book solid enough entertainment for sword-and-sorcery fans but hampered by flaws that would limit its appeal to those with a more rigorous critical eye than the presumably uncritical die-hard fantasy readers.

The ink on those declarations dried long ago. Opinions of A Song of Ice and Fire, like the series itself, continue to evolve in ways that no one could have predicted in 1996. The books have secured a consistent spot atop bestseller lists. They're the source for a hit HBO series. Martin's name can be found on the *Time Magazine* roll call of the planet's most influential people, alongside the likes of Facebook founder Mark Zuckerberg and President Barack Obama.

By the time *A Dance with Dragons* saw publication in 2011, even the *Post* had changed its tune, equating the public anticipation for the new volume with that shown for no less than crossover pop culture phenomenon Harry Potter. The latest Ice and Fire installment was a book, they declared, "with rare—and potentially enormous—appeal." Certainly the sales numbers backed up that claim. The modest first print run for *A Game of Thrones* was a distant memory, with *A Dance with Dragons* shipping several hundred thousand copies in its first week alone. Demand was so great that a sixth printing was ordered even before the official street date. The *Green Bay Gazette* reported that, to satisfy all the new readers, a staggering 4 million copies of the previous books in the series had been printed in just the first half of the year. The HBO adaptation, which had debuted a few months before *A Dance with Dragons* hit shelves, had done much to intensify the buzz, but that exposure alone cannot explain the books' exponentially expanding audience.

A Song of Ice and Fire is not a casual read. To work through a foot-tall stack of purposefully challenging novels requires enough of a commitment that, were the novels not brilliant, the dabblers and the fad-chasers would quickly find some less daunting object for their fickle affection. Martin announces in just about every way possible, from the books' page counts to the long and name-filled appendixes, that they are going to be hard work. Or, at least, they will *appear* to be hard work. One of the most remarkable things about the series is that the short chapters, focused tightly on the various viewpoint characters, make the books immediately accessible in ways everything else about them seems to proclaim unlikely.

That game of confounded expectations is central to the success of A Song of Ice and Fire.

To be clear, labeling this a game is not to suggest it is a mere frivolity. Though there can be a fair bit of dark playfulness in his approach to storytelling, Martin takes it seriously—just as he takes his games seriously. After all, he readily identifies himself as a longtime hobbyist. That interest has led to the creation of several critically acclaimed and smartly realized Ice and Fire-related roleplaying, board, and card games. It informs the title of the first volume in the series and manifests in the works themselves in interesting ways, from the thematic treatment of games—the things the characters view as games, or, more often, mistake as nothing more than diversions, is a variation of the confounded expectations game—to the story's basic structure, with the tightly focused individual chapters functioning quite like the movement of discrete units in a miniatures battle.

On the level of narrative strategy, Martin employs historical and literary allusions and resonances, along with a deceptively open use of genre conventions, to help form reader expectations. Take them too much on face value, though, and you're in for a shock, particularly if your experience with fantasy is dominated by the widely known, consolatory works of J.R.R. Tolkien and C.S. Lewis, where the rightful king is the one who ends up on the throne because the world is, in the end, rational and moral. Martin is just as likely to draw from more obscure weird fantasy writers, or from horror or historical fiction, allowing him to bend genre rules and subvert the same conventions he initially may seem to support. Even HBO got in on this active establishment of false expectations by making Sean Bean's doomed Eddard Stark the literal poster boy for the first season of *Game of Thrones*. It was a knowing wink to viewers familiar with Ned's fate—winter is coming, indeed—and an effective set-up to jolt those experiencing Westeros for the first time through the show.

This narrative strategy also results in texts that are ripe for multiple interpretations and ideal for the sort of discussions we feature in *Beyond the Wall*. In these pages, we explore, among other topics, the characters' clashing perspectives, the mysteries of their pasts and their futures, and the often-confounding moral universe of Westeros and its neighbors. It should come as no surprise that the essayists don't always agree, particularly on the nature, or existence, of the series' moral center. We are, after all, talking about a world in which even the seasons are unreliable. What the gathered writers do share is a love and respect for A Song of Ice and Fire. They offer opinions and critical lenses that suggest new perspectives, vantages that we hope will help you view the works in interesting new ways.

Of course, it's a challenge to write about any series while it is still unfinished, and A Song of Ice and Fire is a particularly difficult work to pin down—and not just for critics. The series started life as a trilogy, after all. That was how Martin's agent first sold it. For a time, five books was the goal, and now it's seven. For the moment, anyway. The story has expanded by thousands of pages past Martin's original target, and the deadline for each new volume's release has become as fluid as its page count. It's been a decidedly messy birth, but that very fact should hearten readers. It means the story is being told as it should be told—as its creator wants it to be told. The chaos is a sign of creative freedom. It shows just how vital, how organic, this magnificent series has become.

"Dead history is writ in ink," notes Roderick "The Reader" Harlaw in *A Feast for Crows*, "the living sort in blood."

The Lord of the Ten Towers may prefer his history dead, but I prefer mine living, thanks very much. My fiction, too. And where A Song of Ice and Fire is concerned, millions of readers around the world—speculative fiction cognoscenti and a much, much larger group devoted simply to brilliant, entertaining storytelling—seem to agree. The purposefully contradictory nature of Westeros and its inhabitants, the tension between the chaotic creative process and George R.R. Martin's controlled, masterful prose, may be messy, may challenge critics and readers alike, but it's also the stuff from which great literature is born.

◆ LINDA ANTONSSON AND ELIO M. GARCÍA, JR. ◆

THE PALACE OF LOVE, THE PALACE OF SORROW

Romanticism in A Song of Ice and Fire

AS WITH ALL THINGS, the passing of time brings changes. The modern fantasy genre has seen trends come and go in the last fifteen years, but one of the most lasting of the recent trends began with the growing success of George R.R. Martin's *A Game of Thrones*. Just as he followed in the footsteps of J.R.R. Tolkien, Stephen R. Donaldson, and more contemporary fantasists such as Robert Jordan and Tad Williams, other authors have been influenced in turn by the traits that Martin's readers associate with his series of novels. Words such as "realistic," "gritty," or "brutal" are terms of reference for many readers when discussing the series, and it can't be denied that these aspects of the story draw a great deal of attention. However, the strength of the novels is not based on literary realism alone. In fact, the realism stands in contrast to another foundational aspect of the narrative: Martin's romanticism.

For some, romanticism may conjure the spectre of bodice-rippers and Harlequin romances. Our meaning when we discuss romanticism in relation to Martin's work is quite specific: an emphasis on emotionality and the individual, a gaze aimed firmly at the past, and a belief in the indomitable human spirit. All of these things were traits of the Romantic movement of the nineteenth century, a movement that Martin has identified himself with in the past. Romanticism has a palpable presence in his award-winning short stories, as well as his novel *Dying of the Light* and especially the antebellum vampire horror novel *Fevre Dream*, in which the Romantic poets Lord Byron and Percy Bysshe Shelley are overtly referenced. Although Martin has said that he feels his earlier work is more romanticist than his later novels, the influence can still be clearly found in the Song of Ice and Fire series, having a pervasive effect on the presentation of the narrative.

The most prevalent manifestation of romanticism is the view of the past espoused by many characters in the novel. It seems a part of human nature to idealize the past, to suppose things were somehow "better" in days gone by. The same can be said about how characters view the past of Westeros, citing examples of how the realm was once better off and has now declined. As one example, the Night's Watch has fallen on hard times. Their numbers are depleted and their cause neglected by most of the great lords and kings, compared to the past when, as Yoren describes it in *A Clash of Kings*, "a man in black was feasted from Dorne to Winterfell, and even high lords called it an honor to shelter him under their roofs."

How true is this statement from Yoren, an older member of the Watch? There's probably some truth to it, but at the same time it seems likely to be a simplification—a simplification revealed when Jon Snow considers some of the history his uncle Benjen taught him, of times past when members of the Watch warred against one another, and when the Starks had to forcibly put the Watch in order. More generally, Jon Snow and others hold a kind of romantic image of the noble calling of the Night's Watch, an image that is swiftly punctured when Tyrion Lannister points out that his brothers will mostly be common thieves and murderers who choose the Wall over death, rather than out of a sense of honor or duty. The Watch has dwindled significantly, with fewer noble-born officers and fewer capable men generally . . . but they certainly were not all high-born paragons even in its earliest days.

The history of the Watch and how it is represented is a subject for an essay all its own, but it makes an easy example. A more central one, however, can be found in the much more recent events of Robert's rebellion—fifteen years in the past in the novels, a bit longer than that in the television series—that most influence the present narrative. The events of that war, both those that led up to it and those that immediately followed, directly touched the lives of nearly every significant character in the series. The melancholic mythologizing with which many characters recall them provide an interesting vantage from which to consider romanticism in the series, as it combines one of the topics Martin generally depicts most viscerally—the violence of war—with the tendency to elide the horrors in favor of poignant remembrances of things lost.

In brief, the fall of the Targaryen dynasty followed on Prince Rhaegar's apparent abduction of Lyanna Stark, then betrothed to Robert Baratheon, and the subsequent murders of Lord Stark and his heir Brandon at the command of King Aerys, the Mad King. This launched a bloody civil war that lasted nearly a year, at the end of which Aerys, Rhaegar, and Rhaegar's wife and children were dead, while the pregnant queen had fled with Aerys's only surviving son and Lyanna died a lonely death in the red mountains of Dorne. The details are parceled out throughout the series, but the very first and strongest link we have to that last event is in the crypt under Winterfell, revealed in one of the very first extended recountings of those events. There King Robert looks on the effigy of Lyanna Stark at her tomb after a moment of solemn silence, and his first words are: "She was more beautiful than that" (*A Game of Thrones*). Immediately, Robert's vision of Lyanna is bound up with the past, with his recollection of her beauty as he remembers it now. Eddard talks of her death, the details of which are vague but bring immediacy by putting the reader in the realm of the senses: a room smelling of "blood and roses"; the whisper of her voice as she pleaded; the clutch of her fingers; the dead, black hue of rose petals that fell from her fingers. The weight of tragedy and loss marking Eddard and Robert is palpable, bound in this shared sense of loss.

But is Robert's vision of Lyanna the same as Eddard's? Later in the first novel, Robert claims Lyanna would never have "shamed" him by questioning his decision to fight in a melee. Eddard responds that Robert did not know Lyanna as well as he did, and what Robert saw was "her beauty, but not the iron

beneath"(*A Game of Thrones*). Finding his vision of Lyanna con-
tradicted leads Robert to refocus the conversation on Eddard's
argument against his participation, leaving Lyanna aside. The
fragility of Robert's romantic vision is a trait that dovetails well
with Robert's morose ambivalence to his station and his duties,
his failures as a man, a husband, and a king weighing on him.
What's most fascinating is the superficiality of Robert's roman-
ticizing of his love for Lyanna, as one comes to realize that if, as
Martin has indicated, Robert spent almost all of his time at the
Vale or Storm's End, he would have had very few occasions to
see Lyanna, much less speak to her. His great passion for her
seems to be in direct proportion to his feeling that she was taken
from him, allowing him an avenue to imagine a Lyanna that
may have had little to do with the actual woman.

Paired with the romantic vision of Lyanna as a tragic figure
is the quite contrasting views we receive of Prince Rhaegar, the
man said to have started the war with his (alleged) abduction of
Lyanna Stark. For Robert, he is a monster who raped Lyanna
until she died, who stole away his betrothed, who deserved to
die a thousand deaths, and who, in the end, won because he and
Lyanna were dead together while Robert lives on as a shadow of
himself. And for Eddard? There's an ambiguity about how Ned
views the Targaryen prince. Ned recalls his victory at Harrenhal,
in a dream of the year of the false spring, seeing Rhaegar carry
the day and then carry the crown for the Queen of Love and
Beauty. When he gave the trophy to Lyanna instead of his wife,
Princess Elia, "all the smiles died" (*A Game of Thrones*). Eddard
compares Rhaegar to Robert at one point, and readers get a hint
that the prince is not seen by Ned the same way as Robert views

him: he doubts Rhaegar would have visited prostitutes and fathered illegitimate children, as his dearest friend and brother has done.

If Lyanna is a figure of personal tragedy that marred the lives of Eddard and Robert, Rhaegar is a more generally tragic figure, one often described in distinctly romantic terms outside of Robert's hearing. Daenerys believes he died for the woman he loved, that he died with her name on his lips. Perhaps more notably, Ser Barristan Selmy offers the following: "He liked to sleep in the ruined hall, beneath the moon and stars, and whenever he came back he would bring a song. When you heard him play his high harp with the silver strings and sing of twilights and tears and the death of kings, you could not but feel that he was singing of himself and those he loved" (*A Storm of Swords*). Not only a romantic figure, but a supremely romantic one at that, because the character seems to have had a premonition of tragedy and doom. The romantic fascination with ruins and decay comes into play in that description, and some of the most vivid imagery in the series has to do with ruins: the Nightfort, Oldstones, Vaes Tolorro, and most certainly Summerhall, the memory of which so strongly shaped Rhaegar's life. The effect of these statements and the notions they've raised in regard to Rhaegar's relationship with Lyanna have had a striking impact on readers. When HBO held a focus group session prior to the airing of *Game of Thrones*, they asked which couples in the show were the "most romantic." Most of the female participants apparently agreed that Lyanna and Rhaegar were the most romantic pairing in the series—a response that must have caused some consternation, as the two were dead characters whose existence is somewhat minimized in the show's first season in comparison to their presence in the novel.

Eddard's own view of Lyanna may be more intimately familiar than it is of Rhaegar, but for him the tragedy of the past is closely tied to the actual tragedy of what befell his family, rather than a self-centered focus on the wrongs done to him. One of the most vivid romantic images in the series, however, directly relates to the events surrounding Lyanna's death: the deadly encounter at the "tower of joy" between Eddard Stark and his six companions against three of the knights of Aerys's Kingsguard. This episode, which closes the war against the Targaryen loyalists, is presented through a feverish dream of Eddard's. The six men who fought beside him—five of whom would not survive—are faceless spectres, despite his efforts to remember them. But the faces of the three knights of the Kingsguard—all famous, and one of them the "splendid" Ser Arthur Dayne, whom Eddard called the "finest knight [he] ever saw" (A Clash of Kings)—are still very clear in his memory. Eddard is haunted by the shadow of the day's events: the deaths of his friends, his own near-death, and the deaths of those three knights who fought and died to honor the vows they had sworn and oaths they had given. As Eddard recalls the words they spoke to one another, the passage reads like a ritualized call and response, lending mythic overtones to this confrontation.

As the warriors rush together, Eddard remembers his sister's scream and the fall of rose petals, and then he wakes. Martin has noted in correspondence that as a dream, not all aspects of the sequence need to be taken literally—a sign, perhaps, that the intrusion of Lyanna into Ned's dream does not represent her

literal presence. But the joining of these two romantic images—
the tragic, doomed sister and the last Kingsguard, who were a
"shining example" to the world—connects these things on a
level that touches on the thematic underpinnings of the series.

Despite the fact that the Kingsguard served Aerys, it's not for
that reason that their reputation is in tatters by the time of *A
Game of Thrones*. What chiefly ended the Kingsguard's place
as the epitome of chivalry and honor in Westerosi thought was
the murder of Aerys by Jaime Lannister. The Kingsguard swore
their lives and honor to defend the king, and Jaime betrayed that
in an utterly unequivocal fashion. Of course, as we delve deeper
into the story, we learn that things are not always as they seem,
that there was more to the events than an arrogant and dishonorable knight advancing his family by betraying the king he'd
sworn to serve. Ser Jaime himself becomes a point-of-view character and reveals that a part of his motivation was to prevent
Aerys from destroying the whole city, and all the lives within
it, out of some mad belief that he'd rise from the ashes in the
body of a dragon. Jaime is ostracized, dubbed the Kingslayer,
reviled—behind his back, in any case—for this ultimate failure,
yet only he knows the whole story.

Moreover, Jaime knows how the Kingsguard themselves
responded to Aerys's madness, when men like the Lord
Commander Ser Gerold Hightower and Ser Jonothor Darry
told him his place was to never judge the king, to never inter-
vene if he sought to harm someone, including his own wife,
unjustly. Yet Jaime keeps these truths bottled up, refusing to
share them out of egoism, so no one will dare *judge* him for having done what he did. This has the effect of making Ser Jaime,

still a Kingsguard, still the handsome, gifted, wealthy son of the wealthiest family in the Seven Kingdoms, an outcast in a society that would normally heap honors and praise on him, but which cannot abide his lack of contrition.

This backstory makes Ser Jaime something very romantic indeed: a Byronic hero. Named for the great Romantic poet Lord Byron, whose characters often exemplified the type, the Byronic hero is "mad, bad, and dangerous to know," and there's a checklist of traits that they often share: cynicism, cunning, disrespect for authority, brilliance, self-destructive behavior, a troubled past, and so on. Once we are in Jaime's head and see him from his perspective, many of these traits coalesce and make it clear that he is not the stock villain that he might have seemed in the first novel. The romanticism of the misunderstood, brilliant man—though Jaime's brilliance is more martial than intellectual, admittedly—is certainly well-attested in period literature. It has survived into modern literature and media, too. There is a certain exceptionalism inherent in romanticism, a focus on the individual as a key figure who needs to be understood to be fully appreciated. The sins of the past might be forgiven, or at least reevaluated, when placed in the fuller context of the character's inner workings.

Jaime's journey through the later novels of the series can be seen as a recapitulation of the journey that Childe Harold takes in Byron's poem, as he escapes a literal prison to enter a different one: the prison of his own actions and reputation. He is constantly judged for what he did and not for why he did it. Now crippled, calling into question both his identity as a warrior *par exellance* and his self-worth, Jaime is led by his decline to reevaluate himself in light of the ideals he once held, the ideals of the youth who wanted to be Ser Arthur Dayne and ended up instead as the outlaw, the Smiling Knight.

Curiously, Jaime's brother Tyrion is also a Byronic figure. Though he lacks the traditional traits of good looks and sexual attractiveness, in most other particulars he fits the definition of the role very well. His outsider position is driven by his physical deformity, which makes him unappealing and the subject of easy mockery, but his status as an outsider is also informed by his public behavior and the very unhappy family situation within which he exists. In a setting where family means everything, the fact that Tyrion's father disregards him, belittles him, and probably hates him is as crippling as being a "grotesque." The result is that Tyrion has become a cynical, jaded figure, incredibly needy for love and attention, but weary of the price he has to pay, sometimes quite literally, to achieve it.

He truly is brilliant, and shows himself capable of enormous feats of ingenuity and command in the course of the novels. And his ultimate reward? Betrayal from his own family, from the woman he thought he loved, from the wife that he tried to love. He's cast out, made an outlaw under penalty of death, and left to fend for himself in a friendless, alien landscape to the east. Tyrion wins over readers through his sharp wit and innate decency, yet he does some terrible things along the way—and still readers forgive him these actions, which seems very much in line with the way Byronic heroes are regarded by those who read about them.

The romanticism of the Lannister brothers and of Robert's rebellion, and the tragedies that these events engendered, can all be connected together by the Great Man Theory of history, which held sway in academic circles during at least some of Martin's college studies. The Great Man Theory is very much a reflection of the Romantic era, in that it supposes the history of the world is largely driven by outstanding individuals initiating world-changing events. This approach to history has fallen out of favor, as Martin himself recounted to a reader when he noted that, during his college days, the "War of the Three Henrys" began to be referred to as the "Wars of Religion," as socioeconomic historiography came to dominate the academic discourse.

Martin's affinity to the theory is less academic and more a matter of pragmatics in storytelling. Readers identify with characters, not socioeconomic trends, so it's natural to position protagonists and antagonists as the primary instigators of events. Social movements take place in the novels—the independent attempt of the "brotherhood without banners" to bring justice to an ugly civil war, the "sparrows" who follow the Seven who gather together to protect one another against the predations of war—but there's always a central individual to provide a focus, even a motivation, as with the "lightning lord" Beric Dondarrion and the nameless septon who's raised up by the mob of sparrows to become High Septon. These individuals provide readers a direct window into these movements, and by studying them one can come to conclusions as to the underlying values and righteousness of their respective causes.

However, the very act of focusing on the individual as a prime instigator of action falls within the pattern of romanticism that Martin has established in the series. Characters are quite directly indicated to be great men: Tywin Lannister is called the greatest man to come along in a thousand years; Robert, during the war, is described in larger-than-life terms; Robb Stark is hailed as the Young Wolf personally responsible for the string of military victories. In every single case, tragedy, disaster, or ignominy— sometimes all three—dogs these characters, and they all meet ugly ends; the high hopes of their beginnings turn to ashes as their lives unravel. No matter how much characters in the Seven Kingdoms, and the readers of the novels, might romanticize these "great men," might romanticize their past and present wars, might find endless virtues to praise, they're all brought down to the earth: Tywin is killed on the privy, Robert's gutted by a boar, Robb Stark is betrayed and his corpse desecrated. Tywin may be the outlier, in that his life was not on a clear decline when he met his sorry end, but for Robb and Robert, we can see that their positions falter and they grow weaker as the disasters mount, swinging inexorably into downward trajectories that are a far cry from their romantic beginnings.

What, then, of the romanticism of A Song of Ice and Fire?

Juxtaposing two quotes from Martin may be useful to close this examination of romanticism. Neither directly touches on it, but together they embody his vision of romanticism. In his brief essay "On Fantasy," Martin explains the purpose of fantasy as he sees it, the reason why he reads it, and why he believes it appeals. At the conclusion, he writes:

> We read fantasy to find the colors again, I think. To taste strong spices and hear the songs the sirens sang. There is something old and true in fantasy that speaks

to something deep within us, to the child who dreamt that one day he would hunt the forests of the night, and feast beneath the hollow hills, and find a love to last forever somewhere south of Oz and north of Shangri-La.

Compare that vision of fantasy to his remarks, in a *Time Magazine* interview, on the topic of decay in his fiction, as related to his family's personal history:

And I think it always gave me this, this sense of a lost golden age of, you know, now we were poor and we lived in the projects and we lived in an apartment. We didn't even have a car, but God we were . . . once we were royalty! It gave me a certain attraction to those kinds of stories of I don't know, fallen civilizations and lost empires and all of that.

Romanticism captures both aspects of Martin's views on fantasy and on stories: it fills the work with another layer of "color" and emotional resonances and a sense of wonder, creating visions of tragic love affairs and doomed nobility, and in turn it highlights the decay of the setting into the gritty reality of the present story. Some of the most memorable scenes in the novels are laden with romanticism, but they're often coupled with an enigma, with the sense that it's a story that's romantic in part because it's not yet been fully told.

Will the tragedy of Lyanna, the doom of Rhaegar, the heroic last stand of the Kingsguard all be revealed as sordid affairs not worth all the paeans and tears? Possibly. Martin has a way of undermining idealizations. But for as long as these romantic visions survive, they enchant readers and facilitate Martin's exploitation of the tension between a reader's hopes for good to happen to characters and the same reader's expectations that nothing good will ever go unspoiled.

◆ ◆ ◆

LINDA ANTONSSON and **ELIO M. GARCÍA, JR.**, met on the internet many years ago, when she was studying Classics at the University of Gothenburg in Sweden and he was studying English literature and medieval history at the University of Miami in Coral Gables. Brought together by a mutual interest in history and fantasy literature, they quickly discovered and were consumed by their fascination with George R.R. Martin's A Song of Ice and Fire series. They first established the Westeros fan site as a means to an end—getting permission from Martin to run a game based on his novels—but from there the scope of the site rapidly grew to become the most expansive repository of information about the series. They have since gone on to host the largest online community dedicated to A Song of Ice and Fire, as well as the largest English-language wiki.

Besides running Westeros.org, Antonsson works as a translator while García works as a freelance writer. They have been involved in a number of Ice and Fire–related projects, including writing articles for websites and magazines, contributing to video and roleplaying games, guest presenting videocasts, and providing creative input on comic book adaptations. They are currently working on The World of Ice and Fire, a guide to the setting co-written with Martin.

◆ ALYSSA ROSENBERG ◆

MEN AND MONSTERS

*Rape, Myth-Making, and the Rise and Fall of Nations
in A Song of Ice and Fire*

THERE'S NO QUESTION THAT the world George R.R. Martin
has created in his Song of Ice and Fire novels is a brutal one,
often novelly so. Whether his characters are being flayed, turned
into zombies in dungeons or ice demons in northern forests, or
burned to death by mad kings and visionary priestesses, there's
no question that life in Westeros and across the narrow sea can
be nasty, brutal, and short. And if you're a woman—and occa-
sionally a man—the threat of sexual assault is omnipresent.

The series' sexual politics have been one of the most-
discussed—and most-misunderstood—aspects of Martin's
books and HBO's adaptation of them. The *New York Times*' Ginia
Bellafante, in her review of the series, wrote that its "costume-
drama sexual hopscotch" suggested that "all of this illicitness

has been tossed in as a little something for the ladies, out of a justifiable fear, perhaps, that no woman alive would watch otherwise." In an (admittedly snarky) discussion of Martin's writing in *A Game of Thrones*, the feminist blogger Sady Doyle wrote that "George R.R. Martin is creepy [...]. He is creepy, primarily, because of his TWENTY THOUSAND MILLION GRATUITOUS RAPE AND/OR MOLESTATION AND/OR DOMESTIC VIOLENCE SCENES."

When writer Rachael Brown asked Martin in a 2011 interview how he decides when to include depictions of sexual violence in his novels, he gave an answer that didn't exactly debunk his critics' arguments:

> I have gotten letters over the years from readers who don't like the sex, they say it's "gratuitous." I think that word gets thrown around and what it seems to mean is "I didn't like it." This person didn't want to read it, so it's gratuitous to that person. And if I'm guilty of having gratuitous sex, then I'm also guilty of having gratuitous violence, and gratuitous feasting, and gratuitous description of clothes, and gratuitous heraldry, because very little of this is necessary to advance the plot.

Martin isn't kidding about the volume of sex scenes and sexual assaults, which show up almost as often as the introduction of a new house crest, if not with the frequency of new dishes at feasts. Despite their frequency, the depictions of sexual assault are often fairly muted, viewed through the lens of painful memory rather than happening in the present tense. For readers who are sensitive to depictions of rape and domestic violence, the number of those assaults or discussions of assault may be an insurmountable barrier to enjoying the books or the show. Everyone has an individual threshhold for violence in art, but it would be a mistake to suggest that depictions of sexual and domestic violence in A Song of Ice and Fire are merely lurid exploitation.

While not all of the sexual assaults that occur in the novels advance the plot, rape is an act that sparks wars and assassinations that reshape continents and the rule of law. And those specific acts that don't impact the larger plot still serve a critically important purpose: attitudes toward sex and consent are one of the ways that citizens of Westeros, the Ironborn, the Free Folk, and members of the societies across the narrow sea distinguish themselves from each other. In Westeros in particular, where the ability to kill is a sign of manhood and even of honor, it's sexual misconduct that signifies monstrosity.

When we're first introduced to the characters whose adventures begin our trek through Martin's expansive world, it's on the occasion of King Robert Baratheon's visit to Winterfell, the holdfast of his old comrade in arms, Ned Stark. Robert justified the war in which he and Ned fought together, and during which he usurped the dynasty that preceded his own, in part because he believes that the heir to that dynasty kidnapped, raped, and killed Lyanna Stark, Ned's sister and the woman Robert was pledged to marry. As he and Ned discuss the war in A Game of Thrones, that alleged atrocity is meant to seal Robert's argument that their campaign was just: "What Aerys did to your brother Brandon was unspeakable. The way your lord father died, that was unspeakable. And Rhaegar . . . how many times do you think he raped your sister? How many *hundreds* of times?"

The defeat of Rhaegar is a personal story for Robert, but it's a fairy tale for the generations to come—they will transmit this tale of sexual violence and revenge to their own children as a way of explaining why Westeros is what, and how, it is. As Bran Stark, Ned's son, tells the other children: "Robert was betrothed to marry her, but Prince Rhaegar carried her off and raped her [. . .]. Robert fought a war to win her back. He killed Rhaegar on the Trident with his hammer, but Lyanna died and he never got her back at all" (*A Game of Thrones*). It's telling that, in this fairy tale, Robert hasn't actually won the world he wanted by staving the prince's chest in. As long as men can carry off the women that other men love, there will be wars of honor—not to mention generation upon generation of women raging under the burden of thwarted sexual and romantic desires. But that sexual violence will be cast as the actions of the monsters, such as Rhaegar.

As the characters fan out from Winterfell, attitudes toward sexual assault become one of the key markers they use to evaluate the new societies they encounter—and to define themselves in relation to those societies. When Jon Snow, Ned Stark's bastard son, joins the Night's Watch—the force of celibate warriors who devote their lives to guarding the massive wall that divides the area of Westeros under the king's control from the wild territories in the land beyond—he's disappointed to learn that his comrades are more criminal than they are willing and noble volunteers. In a vicious cycle, Westeros has come to rely on criminals to populate the Night's Watch, particularly on "rapers," but

then discourages young men of merit from joining the force by
pointing out who they'd be serving alongside. Rapers, because
they can't restrain their sexual impulses, must promise not to be
sexually active again, even as they are physically removed from
greater Westeros as means of holding them to that promise.

Even if the Night's Watch has become a prison colony, a means
of protecting Westeros as much from its own worst citizens as
from its external enemies, when the men of the Watch venture
out, rape again becomes a way that they distinguish themselves
from some of the Free Folk—even their allies. Their first contact
with the Free Folk and last point of refuge is a man called Craster
who has built himself a little holdfast in the woods. When they
first visit his hall, Jon Snow reflects that "Dywen said Craster
was a kinslayer, liar, raper, and craven, and hinted that he traf-
ficked with slavers and demons" (*A Clash of Kings*). To preserve
their relationship with him, and to distinguish themselves from
Craster, Lord Mormont orders the Night's Watch not to touch
his wives (who also happen to be his daughters). On their return
trip, when the order's discipline breaks down, one of the first
things the chaos spawns is the rape of those women, who previously had been considered sacrosanct. These actions mark the
men as traitors and apt targets for the mysterious Coldhands.

Similarly, when Theon Greyjoy, Ned Stark's ward, returns to
his father's court on the Iron Islands, he's ensconced in a society
where rape is a weapon of war. Theon's relatives consider that
which is claimed in battle the only legitimate wealth, so much
so that Theon's father chides him for wearing gold that was
given to him rather than taken forcibly in battle. They regularly
separate their female captives into two classes: women who are

appealing enough to serve as long-term sex slaves, or salt wives, and those unattractive enough to be fit only for physical labor. That attitude toward women—the fact that women are property in the Iron Islands in a way that makes Westeros look like a feminist paradise—is one of the markers set for the reader to show that Theon is in a corrupt and dangerous country.

By contrast, Daenerys Targaryen, a surviving member of the dynasty whose throne Robert Baratheon usurped, lives in exile across the narrow sea from Westeros in Pentos, a continent populated by scattered city-states and nomadic tribes. She attempts to define her rule and distinguish herself from the other petty tyrants she encounters by outlawing rape. Her first attempt to establish these new cultural mores comes when she is still married to Khal Drogo, a powerful warlord among the Dothraki. Daenerys intervenes to restrain Drogo's bodyguards in the aftermath of a successful raid they undertake, in part, to fund her plans to mount an invasion of Westeros and restore the Targaryen dynasty. That intervention earns Daenerys no favors—the woman she saves from assault views her actions as naive paternalism, and it convinces many of Drogo's followers that Daenerys is alienating him from their common values.

After Drogo's death, when Daenerys emerges as a military leader in her own right, her proscriptions against rape may be principled, but they don't eradicate sexual assault in the territories, known as Slaver's Bay, that she conquers. In fact, her efforts to rule compassionately, of which her focus on sexual assault is one aspect, mark Daenerys as a vulnerable ruler, someone who is unable to practice the kind of total war favored by other successful warlords on the continent. It's a tragic testament to the limited power of good intentions in the face of deeply ingrained and intractable cultural practices.

While Daenerys's attempts to reform the sexual culture of Slaver's Bay show her as a civilizing force, one of the clearest signs that Baratheon rule in Westeros is breaking down is the erosion of sexual norms, particularly those that protect noble-women from assault beyond the court. The Lannisters begin to recognize that their position with the common people in King's Landing may truly be untenable after the riot in which Lollys Stokeworth, a minor and not particularly popular member of the court, is gang raped by more than fifty men. Her assault is a sign of how deep the public contempt for the regime runs.

Sexual violence also plays a role in court politics and is often used in the narrative to show just how deeply the nobility is sep-arated from its ideals. King Robert dies, poisoned by his queen, Cersei Lannister, who is seeking retaliation for the marital rape and domestic violence to which Robert regularly subjected her in violation of chivalric ideals. His son Joffrey succeeds him, and promptly intensifies that dynamic of abuse and makes it public. Sansa Stark, Ned's daughter, who is engaged to Joffrey, was once excited by the prospects of the match. But after Ned's death, Joffrey reveals himself to be a sexual sadist. Sansa is stripped and beaten by Joffrey's bodyguards. Having his men perpetrate the abuse technically absolves him from direct blame for hitting her, but it also makes the knights complicit in the assault and forces them to choose between obeying his orders and beating a woman. Though he never makes good on his promise, Joffrey repeatedly threatens to rape Sansa, even after he marries her off to his uncle Tyrion.

Tyrion himself is a victim and perpetrator of sexual abuse: his own father orders his commoner wife gang raped to punish Tyrion, even forcing Tyrion to participate. It's not the first time rape is utilized as a weapon in the poisonous Lannister family dynamic. After Cersei believes she's discovered Tyrion's mistress and taken her captive, Tyrion threatens to hold her son hostage against Cersei's promise of the woman's safety. "Whatever happens to her happens to Tommen as well, and that includes the beatings and rapes," he tells his sister, thinking, "*If she thinks me such a monster, I'll play the part for her*" (*A Clash of Kings*).

Sexual violence is also the hallmark of, perhaps, the two greatest monsters to appear in the series to date: the freakishly large Gregor Clegane, the Mountain That Rides, and Ramsay Bolton, the legitimated son of Roose Bolton, Lord of the Dreadfort.

There are many rumors about Gregor Clegane's brutality, but the one act that defines his monstrosity is the rape and murder of Elia Targaryen, along with the murder of her son. The story of Gregor's atrocities against Elia is told over and over again in the series, from multiple perspectives. It's one of the first things that Ned recalls about the man when he comes to court in *A Game of Thrones*. In a litany of possible crimes involving dead siblings, mysterious fires, and disappearing servants, the story of Elia's rape and murder is the most specific charge against Gregor. It is the moment when he stepped over the line, exceeding his orders to kill the last of the Targaryen line and moving beyond the kind of domestic brutality Westerosi society tolerates, as long as it is kept private, into overt villainy.

While the people who benefit from Gregor's atrocities may appreciate the end results and grudgingly accept that it's necessary for someone to perform such violent acts, his brutality still makes them intensely uncomfortable. In *A Storm of Swords*, Tywin Lannister, who has never felt the need to justify anything to his youngest son Tyrion, makes an exception to that general contempt to try to explain how such a thing could have taken place while he was in command of the army: "I grant you, it was done too brutally," he admits. "I did not tell him to spare her. I doubt I mentioned her at all. I had more pressing concerns [. . .]. Nor did I yet grasp what I had in Gregor Clegane, only that he was huge and terrible in battle." He's willing to confess to having ordered the family assassinated, but the suggestion that he ordered Clegane to assault Elia is something he rejects: "The rape . . . even you will not accuse me of giving *that* command, I would hope."

It seems, for a moment, that the monsterous Mountain will be defeated by a hero when Oberyn Martell, the foreign prince who was Elia's brother, faces Gregor in trial by combat. During the duel itself, Oberyn's taunts unnerve Gregor into making a confession. Yet he answers his rival in a way that feels more like a triumphant reaffirmation of the act than a repudiation of it:

> "I killed her screaming whelp." He thrust his free hand into Oberyn's unprotected face, pushing steel fingers into his eyes. "*Then* I raped her." Clegane slammed his fist into the Dornishman's mouth, making splinters of his teeth. "Then I smashed her fucking head in. Like this." As he drew back his huge fist, the blood on his gauntlet seemed to smoke in the cold dawn air. There was a sickening *crunch*. (*A Storm of Swords*)

It's a monstrous way to end a fight, and one that forces polite Westerosi society to acknowledge what kind of beast they've tolerated in their midst all these years. They could ignore Clegane's atrocities while he himself was quiet about them. His public affirmation of his guilt, though, indicts the nobility for harboring him.

The duel marks Gregor's transformation into a literal monster. Though the Mountain manages to kill Oberyn, the Red Viper poisons Gregor before he dies. The defrocked Maester Qyburn takes Gregor into his lab and proceeds to turn him into an unbeatable champion, murdering inconvenient members of the court so he can harvest their organs for his own use. There's an extent to which these developments are afterthoughts, emphasis added to a fact that was already established long ago: Gregor Clegane needed no help from anyone to become a monster; the violence he perpetrated against Elia established him as monstrous long ago.

While Gregor's crimes began before the events of the first novel in the series, we witness the full empowerment of another horror, whose atrocities against women are directly linked to his rising acceptance in Westerosi society. The first thing we know about Ramsay Bolton, born a bastard but legitimated by his father, is that he abuses his wife. After he is recognized by his father, Ramsay marries Lady Hornwood to gain control of her ancestral house, then leaves her to starve to death in a tower cell. As the story of her death spreads, the detail that stands out is that she chewed off her own fingers in her desperate search for sustenance before death finally claimed her.

His abuse of women is both widespread and notorious. As one nobleman explains to another, the Bastard of the Dreadfort takes up the unpleasant habit of hunting down women in whom he's interested: "When Ramsay catches them he rapes them, flays them, feeds their corpses to his dogs, and brings their skins back to the Dreadfort as trophies. If they have given him good sport, he slits their throats before he skins them. Elsewise, t'other way around" (*A Dance with Dragons*).

When Theon Greyjoy falls under Ramsay's control, the sadist gelds him, partially flays him, and forces Theon to participate in sexual assaults, most notably on a servant who is impersonating the late Ned Stark's younger daughter, Arya. So while women are not Ramsay's only victims, his crimes sooner or later seem to involve them.

Eventually we learn that the Bastard of the Dreadfort is, himself, the product of sexual violence. Roose Bolton raped Ramsay's mother in an exercise of his first night rights, a story he relates in *A Dance with Dragons* with a casualness that's chilling:

"I was hunting a fox along the Weeping Water when I chanced upon a mill and saw a young woman washing clothes in the stream. The old miller had gotten himself a new young wife, a girl not half his age. She was a tall, willowy creature, very *healthy*-looking. Long legs and small firm breasts, like two ripe plums. Pretty, in a common sort of way. The moment that I set eyes on her I wanted her. Such was my due. The maesters will tell you that King Jaehaerys abolished the lord's right to the first night to appease his shrewish queen, but where the old gods rule, old customs linger [. . .]. So I had him hanged, and claimed my rights beneath the tree where he was swaying. If truth be told, the wench was hardly worth the rope. The fox escaped as well, and on our way back to the Dreadfort my favorite courser came up lame, so all in all it was a dismal day."

In *A Storm of Swords*, Roose admits to Catelyn Stark that Ramsay's "blood is tainted, that cannot be denied." While he undoubtedly means that his line has been polluted by having to divert it through an illegitimate son who is half-peasant, Robett Glover provides an alternative explanation in *A Dance with Dragons*: "The evil is in his blood. He is a bastard born of rape. A *Snow*, no matter what the boy king says." While it may be decidedly antimodern to blame children who are the product of rape for his parents' sins, there's something to the idea that unpunished rape is a sin that carries implications far beyond individual victims and perpetrators, a crime that comes back to haunt the society that permits and enables it. This is the one moment in the novels when the characters acknowledge an argument that Martin's been building for us all along: rape produces damage that lingers beyond a single act, a single victim. It can produce monsters that contribute to the destabilization of entire societies.

Rape touches the lives, and shapes the world, of almost all the characters in the series, be they noble or common-born, perpetrators or victims. And while each of them feels pain, and terror, and anger individually, it's given to us to see the collective impact of these assaults across continents. Even when rape isn't being used as excuse to start a war or a way to manipulate court politics, a tolerance for rape and the failure to provide justice to its victims deforms Westeros and its enemies alike. Rather than an exercise in exploitation, the pervasive nature of sexual violence in A Song of Ice and Fire serves as a powerful indication, and indictment, of corruption and inhumanity.

◆ ◆ ◆

ALYSSA ROSENBERG is the culture blogger at ThinkProgress, and the television correspondent for *The Atlantic*, where she writes regularly on gender, race, and the presentation of policy issues in popular culture. Her work has appeared in Esquire.com, The Daily, *The American Prospect*, *The Washington Monthly*, *The New Republic*, *National Journal*, and The Daily Beast. She lives in Washington, D.C.

◆ DANIEL ABRAHAM ◆

SAME SONG IN A DIFFERENT KEY

Adapting A Game of Thrones *as a Graphic Novel*

WHEN I WAS FIRST approached about adapting *A Game of Thrones* to graphic novel form, Anne Groell, the editor who has overseen these books from the start, asked me to write a brief philosophical statement on my approach to the project. It's been said that no plan survives contact with the enemy. No adaptor's philosophical statement does either. The opinion I worked out in the page and a half I gave her hasn't been unmade by the experience of working through the scripts, but it's been tested and refined and become generally better fleshed out.

Let me give you a little background.

When it comes to prose, I believe that reading is an essentially performative act, where directions given by the author are interpreted by the reader in a series of deeply personal, private, and unshareable acts of imagination. When George R.R. Martin writes something like, "The gods of Winterfell kept a different sort of wood. It was a dark, primal place, three acres of old forest untouched for a thousand years as the gloomy castle rose around it" (*A Game of Thrones*), each of us as readers comes up with a set of images and smells and abstract emotions that make up that experience for us. For me, there's a sense of darkness and greenness and buildings glimpsed between tree trunks. Someone else might have more familiarity with oak trees and the smell of forest litter. There's no reason to think that the things conjured by the text are the same for everyone—they almost certainly aren't. And the way that we tailor those scenes and images makes up our experience of the story. That's what we mean when we talk about the literary dream. Graphic novels— comic books, sequential art, however you choose to describe the medium—employs different tools to achieve an effect similar to prose, but it's not identical.

In one way, graphic novels require less cognitive effort from the audience than prose. By providing images to the reader, graphic novels give the creators more control over the immediate visual aspects of the reader's private, internal experience, but also lose some of the less concrete information control that prose offers with, for example, exposition, which we'll talk about specifically later on. The idiom that creates the story has different strengths, different relationships to information control, and moving from one toolbox to the other isn't trivial. Because the experience of the tale is shaped by the tools used in the telling, what exactly is being preserved in the translation is a critically important question. An adaptation that tries to recapture the experience of coming to a story for the first time, another that recreates the thematic and artistic intentions (as understood by the adapting team), and a third that cleaves as closely as possible to the actions described in the text, can all be faithful to a source without being at all similar to one another. There was never any question that, in adapting *A Game of Thrones*, we should be true to the spirit of the original book, but what exactly that fidelity meant had some pretty wide error bars.

Refining and defining what it meant to keep faith with the original was bounded by two kinds of considerations: specific, concrete problems idiosyncratic to *A Game of Thrones* on the one hand, and structural issues that rise from the act of moving between prose and graphic storytelling regardless of the underlying work on the other. I'll give some examples of each.

The first of the idiosyncratic issues was the place A Song of Ice and Fire had achieved in the cultural moment. Our adaptation of *A Game of Thrones* wasn't the first one that the books had inspired. Before our comic book project began, there had already been replica swords, sculptures, and enough art to fill several calendars, card and board games, and two volumes of *The Art of George R.R. Martin's A Song of Ice and Fire*. The popularity of the novels had also inspired a television series that was already casting. Which is to say, *A Game of Thrones* was already in the center of a body of artistic work that had spread well beyond the book itself. How we chose to play off those existing visions of the characters, places, and events had practical implications for more than just us.

There is an attraction to participating in a larger creative enterprise. If our Eddard Stark bore some resemblance to the actor cast in the television show, the image would gain something by the familiarity. Ted Naismith did brilliant versions of Winterfell and the Eyrie. John Picacio's Eddard Stark, Jon Snow, and Daenerys Targaryen are wonderfully realized and compelling. These talented people have already created a bevy of first-class work. Why not build on what they've accomplished? The artistic argument against that strategy was that, in taking our lead from earlier artists, we would sacrifice something of our own originality and vision. By tying ourselves to what had come before, we would lose the opportunity to invent our own versions, maybe better, maybe not, but certainly more authentically our own. Neither was that the only consideration.

As much as I would like to think that artistic concerns are first and last in all things, the constraints on a project are rarely exclusively aesthetic. The property for which we had rights was, and is, the original novel. While it would be possible to get the permission from the previous artists who had created versions of Westeros, keeping track of the full catalog of A Song of Ice and Fire creations and integrating them into our version of the story could prove more awkward, time-consuming, and unwieldy than starting from scratch. There would necessarily be some family resemblances among the various incarnations of *A Game of Thrones*. We are, after all, interpreting the same source material and sometimes artists naturally reach for the same solutions to common problems. And there were some real problems. For example, Daenerys.

Daenerys Targaryen was the second issue that we faced, one specific to *A Game of Thrones*, and very thorny, both for us and for other adaptors. Her character arc in the book takes her from emotionally abused political pawn, through an arranged marriage that rightly lifts the ethical hackles of a contemporary readership, an overtly sexual coming-of-age, a pregnancy, and a miscarriage, to become a political leader and powerful force in her own right. Her sexual awakening and the relationship of her sexuality to power are central to her story, as are issues of consent, control, and fertility. At the beginning of the book, she is thirteen years old.

There is an argument that drawing the story as it is written would be *illegal*.

The PROTECT Act of 2003 prohibits "obscene visual depiction of a minor engaging in sexually explicit conduct" where the term "obscene" is defined according to the Miller Test. That is, a work can be classed as obscene if it violates community standards, is patently offensive, and, as a whole, lacks literary or artistic value. Whether the comic would have met those standards would be for a court to determine, unless we did something that explicitly took into account the legal implications of moving from text to image. The television adaptation addressed this by casting an actress who was legally of age. The comic book has no actress, and so the images created of her don't have an objective truth to use in their defense. The alternatives available were either to omit several of the most important character moments, change the age of the character to fit contemporary legal standards regardless of the violence that would do to the intent of the story, or remain utterly faithful to the original text and prepare for scandal, censure, and legal action.

The third issue that *A Game of Thrones* brought with it was that A Song of Ice and Fire is still in progress. In the previous adaptations I've done—of the novel *Fevre Dream* and the novella "The Skin Trade"—there has been a finalized story in print. By knowing the ending toward which the plot was progressing, it becomes possible to see how events were foreshadowed in the text, and how that could be recreated in images. *A Game of Thrones*, on the other hand, is the first book in a series that is expected to run seven volumes, the last three of which hadn't been published when the first scripts were written for the graphic novel. A Song of Ice and Fire is also notable for its willingness to surprise and work against the expectations of the genre. Knowing which characters are important to the overall story—and even which ones will survive to the final volume—is almost impossible at this stage. When Robb Stark and Jon Snow find the direwolf pups, Eddard Stark's full group is with them, something like eight or ten named characters. Drawing them all could be visually confusing and cluttered. But the fact that Theon Greyjoy was present may be important later on. What can be cut and what can't simply isn't obvious yet.

That's not true for every project. There are certainly long-running comic book series that have succeeded brilliantly without a strict continuity or foreshadowing that began years ahead. I'm thinking of ongoing serial (even soap-operatic) titles such as *Batman* or *Spider-Man*. But A Song of Ice and Fire isn't open-ended. It does have a conclusion it moves toward, and in fact, the last sentence of the last book is already decided. Adapting the story without having the full text to judge still allows approaches ranging from strict adherence to the source material, to a good faith "best guess" on the adaptor's part, to gathering information from lengthy interviews with George. It's even possible to imagine an adaptation in which the ending of the graphic novels isn't the same as the ending of the books, the two versions diverging as they progress, each controlled by its own internal logic. At that point, though, what exactly the adaptor is preserving rightly comes into question.

So, in addition to the peculiar issues of *A Game of Thrones*, there are more general structural differences between prose and sequential art that constrain the boundaries of adaptation. These grow, for the most part, from the aural nature of written English.

The literal symbols of English writing are encodings of sound, not vision. When reading prose silently, the sensual experience most immediately and easily evoked is sound, and the sound most easily evoked is the spoken voice of the characters or the narrator. This makes dialogue one of the strengths of prose fiction.

Reading well-crafted dialogue is like eavesdropping. A few telling physical details and small actions are enough to let the reader create a full, complex, and satisfying experience of the scene; Viserys's lilac eyes as he sniffs disdainfully at Dany's gift of Dothraki clothing and Eddard testing Needle's edge with his thumb during his talk with Arya happen within the context of longer conversations, and not every exchange includes details like these. Graphic novels, by contrast, require a full visual component, and the natural fit for two people having a conversation—a long series of pictures of the person or people talking—gets dull fast. Dialogue that crackles with life and vitality in prose gets tedious when it's rendered as page after page filled with pictures of talking heads and staggered word balloons. In a project that relies on dialogue—and most novels rely on dialogue—reframing the action so that more of the information is given to the reader through images is a challenge, and it encourages the adaptor to reimagine the scenes in ways that simplify and condense conversations, while amplifying action and the images that take the place of physical description in prose, even when that means doing some violence to the story.

Narrative voice is also a serious and related structural issue in the translation between media. It also brings in the collaborative nature of the adaptation. In prose, the narrator is an additional and often unnamed character with an idiosyncratic voice and manner that sets the essential tone of the story and provides information to the reader. In transitioning to comic books, those two functions are split.

The basic feel of a comic book isn't provided by the narrator's imagined speaking voice but by the artist's visual style. Whether we are to take a story—or even a scene within a story—seriously or lightly is signaled by the way in which it is drawn and the palate used in coloring it. This is very similar to the way that word choices and vocal rhythms of a narrator's voice cue a reader how to interpret action in prose. Imagine, for example, Winterfell drawn as a Disney princess cartoon as opposed to the style of Ted Naismith. The way that the artist approaches the image *is* the mood of the piece and exists with its own set of constraints, including the skill and interests of the artist and the time pressure of production. While the scripter can specify that an image be more stylized or realistic and describe the effect that an image or scene should convey, the actual drawing has to rely on the skill and, more importantly, the judgment of the artist. The images, however carefully conceived by the person making the script, are the necessary subject of the person drawing the lines, and the choices made at the drawing table are as important as the ones made at the keyboard. The role of the narrative voice as a cue on how to approach the project is actually taken out of the writer's hands. Even if the script gives lengthy, specific instructions to the artist in the best Alan Moore tradition, the artist will still interpret it and make decisions that sometimes differ from the script. But what the visual style can't do that a prose narrator can is provide abstract information, like exposition.

Exposition is always a problem. How well an author manages exposition is one good litmus test for quality. By having an engaging narrative voice, a text can move away from the literal and concrete action in a scene—the cinematic aspects of the story—to give background information, history, or philosophical and thematic grounding. *A Game of Thrones* in particular features passages that cover the history of Westeros and the complex backstories of the characters engaged in conversation in the scenes. When Eddard and Robert descend to the crypt below Winterfell to visit Lyanna's grave, for example, there's a wealth of information in the text about how the three of them were related, how Brandon Stark and the Tullys fit in, and the history of the rebellion that put Robert on the throne. There is no graceful way to take that abstract information and present it in a purely visual form. The options are to reprint the prose exposition (either entirely or in summary) with some limited illustration, omit the exposition and lose the depth and background, or take the information that was presented in exposition and shoehorn it into the action of the story, often using dialogue, with all the attendant trouble that creates.

A third strictly technical issue is the pacing of the plot. *A Game of Thrones* is built in chapters of varying lengths with the dramatic high points and resting places coming where they fit organically within those units, both individually and combined as a full novel. Recasting the same tale as a series of four graphic novels requires that the dramatic high points fall evenly and the quarter, half, three-quarter, and end marks even to the specific page. Furthermore, since each of the graphic novels is a concatenation of six comic book issues, lesser concluding moments come in at regular and prescribed intervals, which may or may not coincide with the source material.

We had some freedom in shaping the project at the beginning, when the structure was being set. The decisions made at that juncture—how many issues of the comic book would there be, how many pages in each issue, how many issues would be gathered into each graphic novel, how many graphic novels would there be—affected every subsequent decision. *A Game of Thrones* could be condensed and simplified down viciously by omitting subplots, characters, and scenes, rewriting characters' relationships and motivations. It could also be expanded out into an epic to rival the original *Akira*, with the art being given more territory to expand and the more visual scenes playing out over the course of pages rather than panels. Either approach could be good, but they couldn't be equivalent, and how each of the other decisions played out would be impacted by the shape of the scaffold erected in those early meetings.

So with those specific issues as a kind of sampler, we can come back again to the central question: when adapting from prose to sequential art, what am I trying to preserve and what am I willing to sacrifice?

It would be great if all the issues militated for one answer, but in practice, any one concern can find another that seems to oppose it. If I remain faithful to the original story, I face the problem of how to preserve the exposition, the dialogue, and the age of the younger characters. If I let the original story fall by the wayside and reimagine Westeros—adding new characters and plotlines or recreating ones that already exist—I have to confront the unfinished nature of the original and the expectations from the reader based on the novel and the other adaptations.

The first extreme, and the one that is in some ways the most tempting, is to preserve not the story itself, but the sense of wonder and grandeur and scope that comes from reading *A Game of Thrones* for the first time. A Song of Ice and Fire has been described as an epic retelling of the War of the Roses without the burden of history. Would it really be a violation of the spirit, then, for the graphic novel version to be a retelling of *A Game of Thrones* without the burden of the novel? If we rebooted Westeros, took the names and general plot, but changed the details and their echoes, and let the story as told in the graphic novels become its own tale, it would also participate in a long-standing tradition inside comics. How many versions of the Batman story have been told without doing violence to the underlying creation of Bob Kane?

The other extreme approach would be to remain perfectly faithful to the original text. One editor called this the "Classics Illustrated" approach. Where there are stretches of exposition or dialogue that didn't fit gracefully into a visual composition, put in pages of the original text, perhaps illuminated like a medieval manuscript. Risk legal action with the underage sexuality, or else replace the images with the original text and leave the rest to the audience's imagination. In this version, the graphic novels become less of an independent project and more of a special edition of the original book. The problem of not knowing what happens in the final, unwritten volumes of the series is solved by including everything, no matter how apparently insignificant.

In practice, the course we'll take will rest between the two options, but nearer—and I think significantly nearer—to one than the other. Charting our best course depends on what *A Game of Thrones* in particular and A Song of Ice and Fire in the larger scheme *is*.

And we don't know that yet.

For me, the single most important fact about A Song of Ice and Fire is that it will end. Daenerys Targaryen will have a last scene and a last word. Because of my participation in this project, I know the fate of several major characters, and have a good idea of the final plot arc. Even so, the details of where the many, many characters end—where, in fact, Westeros itself ends—aren't all available to me. They may not even be available to George.

My experience writing my own novels suggests that even at this late stage in the project, the best writers are in an ongoing process of discovery. Even with the last scenes firmly in mind, the process of reaching that place is full of surprises. Some of the ideas and intentions for *The Winds of Winter* and *A Dream of Spring* will change in the telling of the tale, because that is the inevitable process of creation. Especially as we near the end, the events at the beginning will take on new significance. Prophecies will unfold in ways that may be as surprising to the author as they are to the reader. Things that are foreshadowed will come to be, or else they won't. Until the ending comes, recreating Westeros—adding new characters, remaking old ones, taking action from perspectives different from those already in the books—isn't an act of translation or adaptation. It's just making things up.

It's possible that once the whole project is complete, a faithful adaptation could be done at some greater level of abstraction. The story of Tyrion Lannister could be rewritten in a way that serves the same overall function in this different medium. The effect of Viserys's or Drogo's deaths on Daenerys could be reached in some other way that was still true to the character that she is presently still in the process of becoming. Until the tale is told through to its ending, those deeper levels are still unavailable for judgment or consideration. Recreating Westeros as George intends it to be may not always be impossible, but it is at the moment.

I remember reading an essay about the art of copying paintings, especially as it is practiced in China. The epitome of that art, the writer argued, was the invisibility of the copier. Ideally, the reproduction and the original should be indistinguishable. I've thought about that aesthetic often in the course of adapting *A Game of Thrones*. In most of my professional career, my job has been to create and present my own vision as clearly and powerfully as I could. I like to think that my own novels carry my vision to readers in ways that are idiosyncratic to me.

I imagine myself as the painter of some original work. In adapting, I become a copier.

The constraints on how I can do it are real. I have chosen to age Daenerys up to match our legal standards, even though it means telling the story of an immature, controlled, and sheltered young woman rather than a powerful, exploited, and complex child. I have summarized conversations and removed exposition that worked very well in the book because I thought it wouldn't work in the new format. I've reordered some chapters and actions to better fit the page counts of the comic books and the collected graphic novels. But the guiding principle is always—and necessarily—that the reader of this new work see Tommy Patterson's art and George R.R. Martin's story. My job is to be invisible. If no one sees or considers the decisions I've made and instead they fall into George's story and Tommy's art, I will have succeeded.

◆ ◆ ◆

DANIEL ABRAHAM is the nationally bestselling author of thirteen novels and thirty short stories, including the critically acclaimed Long Price Quartet and *Hunter's Run* (with George R.R. Martin and Gardner Dozois). He also writes as M.L.N. Hanover and (with Ty Franck) as James S.A. Corey. He has been nominated for the Hugo, Nebula, and World Fantasy Awards, and been awarded the International Horror Guild Award. His current projects include the epic fantasy series The Dagger and the Coin, the space opera series The Expanse, and the ongoing urban fantasy series The Black Sun's Daughter. He also writes occasional nonfiction columns for io9, SF Signal, and *Clarkesworld*.

◆ ADAM WHITEHEAD ◆

AN UNRELIABLE WORLD

History and Timekeeping in Westeros

IN ANY SETTING WITH a complex history and mythology, it is common for the author to reveal and explore the backstory at the same time the main storyline is driving forward. This is true in A Song of Ice and Fire, where even as the central plot unfolds and we witness Westeros's descent into the chaos of the War of the Five Kings and Daenerys Targaryen's tribulations in the distant east, we learn more about the events that came before. We learn about the reign of the Mad King, the Targaryen conquest, the flight of the Rhoynar to Dorne, and the raising of the Wall to defend against the Others. Even as the story moves ahead, it also moves back, giving more depth and resonance to current events by showing how they were set up decades, centuries, or even millennia earlier. But we also learn that the accounts of time and history in the books are not to be trusted, with doubts raised over when events happened, or even if they ever happened at all.

Tracking the Years

One of the defining characteristics of the setting for A Song of Ice and Fire is that the seasons last for years at a time and are unpredictable: a decade-long winter can be followed by a substantially shorter summer. As well as introducing logistical difficulties for the characters of Westeros, it also causes problems for the tracking of history and time. In A Song of Ice and Fire, characters live in a world whose very history is uncertain and ill-defined, where myth and legend are hopelessly and inextricably entwined with accounts of real events. The predominant feature of Westerosi history is vagueness.

Early in A Game of Thrones we are shown the Wall, a vast edifice that stretches across the northern border of the Seven Kingdoms and holds back the threats that lurk beyond, both supernatural and mundane. We are told that the Wall is eight thousand years old. This is a vast number, enough to give even hardened fantasy readers pause. In reality, eight thousand years is almost twice the age of the Great Pyramids, and even with modern archaeological techniques our knowledge of our own comparable historical period (c. 6000 B.C.) is sketchy at best. In a fantasy world lacking such technology, where frequent long winters threaten to destroy civilization entirely, the notion that these people would have any idea what happened eight thousand years earlier seems fanciful.

Some critics have complained about the vast spans of time referenced in the series, calling them "unrealistic." This criticism is answered—or at least addressed—in the text itself. The spans of time are vast, but they may also be illusory. Over the centuries, tradition and myth petrify into accepted fact; the truth may be very different, in this case, involving much shorter spans of time. When Jon Snow sends Samwell Tarly to research the history of the Night's Watch in an effort to learn more about the Others, a confused Samwell reports that the number of Lord Commanders to which he can find references is far smaller than less formal histories suggest.

> "The oldest histories we have were written after the Andals came to Westeros. The First Men only left us runes on rocks, so everything we think we know about the Age of Heroes and the Dawn Age and the Long Night comes from accounts set down by septons thousands of years later [. . .]. Those old histories are full of kings who reigned for hundreds of years, and knights riding around a thousand years before there *were* knights. You know the tales [. . .] we say that you're the nine hundred and ninety-eighth Lord Commander of the Night's Watch, but the oldest list I've found shows six hundred seventy-four commanders." (*A Feast for Crows*)

This is an important statement, confirming the notion that the history of the Seven Kingdoms is based on myths and legends much more than on hard historical facts. Before the Andals came to Westeros, the First Men used runes chiselled into rocks and oral storytelling traditions to pass information on from one generation to the next. There may be some truth in these stories—some of Homer's account of the Trojan War in *The Iliad*, drawn from older, oral traditions in our world, has been backed up by archaeological findings at the real site of Troy, for example—but there is also a lot of hyperbole and fantastical invention. Even the Andals' historical records are inexact and prone to creative flourishes and outright errors, especially since even their arrival in Westeros is impossible to date reliably. "[N]o one knows when the Andals crossed the narrow sea," Hoster Blackwood explains in *A Dance with Dragons*. "The *True History* says four thousand years have passed since then, but some maesters claim that it was only two. Past a certain point, all the dates grow hazy and confused, and the clarity of history becomes the fog of legend."

It's worth noting that the appendix to *A Game of Thrones* actually suggests six thousand years have passed since the Andals' arrival, whilst Hoster Blackwood's remarks to Jaime in *A Dance with Dragons* suggest it could be as little as two thousand. An "error margin" of some four thousand years leaves significant room for doubts, mistakes, and miscalculations.

Seasons of Uncertainty

The enormous difficulty in calculating history in Westeros is down to the lack of regular seasons. When one season might last for a few months and the next for years, records of harvests, plantings, summer festivals, and so on become highly unreliable. Even the maesters of the Citadel, with their exacting measurements and timelines, find themselves arguing over dates and details. Neither has it been revealed in the books how long the maesters or the Citadel have been around. They are just one more example of the fog of uncertainty shrouding the entire backstory of Westeros—one more example of how history itself is an unreliable narrator in the series.

The unpredictable seasons also answer another common criticism about technological stasis in Westeros. The kingdoms in A Song of Ice and Fire have seen historical epochs pass much as in real history, just at a slower rate. We are told that the First Men brought bronze to Westeros some twelve thousand years before the start of the books. By tradition—which, as we have already seen, may not be entirely reliable—the Andals followed with iron and horse-riding some six thousand years later. In reality, the Bronze Age in Europe lasted from roughly 3200 to 600 B.C., a period of twenty-six centuries. The following Iron Age overlapped it, extending from 1200 A.D. to 400 B.C., a period of sixteen centuries. If we take into account the slowing of technological progress due to the long winters, effectively mini ice ages occurring up to several times a century, the corresponding technological ages in Westeros only last two to three times longer than their real-life counterparts.

That said, we are also given conflicting information about technological and sociological matters: the appendix to A Game of Thrones tells us that the Andals brought the concept of chivalry to Westeros, but in A Feast for Crows, Samwell Tarly suggests that the institution of knighthood is a more recent one and highlights the fact that some stories speak of knights living a thousand years before they could have existed. This is, of course, a nod to the legend of King Arthur, where knights in the medieval tradition are depicted as living and fighting a clear half-millennia before such fighting men came into being.

A wild card in this matter is the existence of magic. The degree to which magic was practiced in Westeros before the Doom of Valyria is unclear, but certainly at one time magic was used for formidable tasks, such as the raising of the Wall and the building of Storm's End. The notion that magic retards technological development, if not preventing it altogether, is a common conceit in epic fantasy. Magic in Westeros, even when used, was not as prevalent as in other fantasy stories, and its use may have helped slow, but not prevent, technological advancement. This conflict between magic and science is given a clearer definition in *A Feast for Crows*, when we are told that the maesters of the Citadel believe that magic should be made obsolete and stamped out wherever it is encountered for the benefit of science.

The backstory to A Song of Ice and Fire thus lacks definition up until the arrival of Aegon the Conqueror in Westeros, a mere three centuries before the start of the series. At this point history suddenly snaps into focus, and we get hard dates for the reigns of the Targaryen kings and major events that happen during their reign. Before that, history is less hard fact and more shifting legend.

History on a Personal Scale

This unreliability of history extends onto a more personal scale as well. Characters are defined by their experiences and what has happened to them in the past, as well as by their families and their family histories. These histories themselves often suffer from uncertainty as much as the larger-scale timeline. Jon Snow, a major protagonist of the series—if not *the* major protagonist—is a character uncertain of his own identity; he doesn't know anything at all about his real mother, not even her name. Cruelly, he is not privy to information that the reader and even other characters possess. Catelyn Stark never told him about the rumors that his mother might be Ashara Dayne of Starfall, and Arya has not been able to tell him that his mother might be the Dayne servant,

Wylla, as revealed to her by Edric Dayne in *A Storm of Swords*. This latter point is crucial, as Wylla was identified by Eddard Stark as Jon's mother to his best friend, Robert Baratheon.

This mystery is at the heart of the series, gaining more power as readers learn that Eddard Stark might not even be Jon's father in the first place. In this instance we are given conflicting information from multiple sources about the matter. Jon may be the son of Eddard and Ashara, or Eddard and Wylla, or Eddard and an unknown fisherman's daughter from the Vale of Arryn. Or he may not be Eddard's son at all but a child of Rhaegar Targaryen and Lyanna Stark, claimed by Eddard to protect him from Robert Baratheon's fury. Of course, if he were the son of Rhaegar and Lyanna, he would be illegitimate . . . unless his parents had secretly married. Since Targaryens could take multiple wives and all of their offspring would have a claim as heirs, this could theoretically give Jon a claim to the throne, although one that would be very hard to prove.

Going back further, even the story of Rhaegar and Lyanna's relationship is clouded by mystery. Robert Baratheon believes that Rhaegar abducted and raped Lyanna. Eddard is less sure. Later, in *A Storm of Swords*, Howland Reed's children seem to tell Bran that the relationship between the two began more romantically, with Lyanna weeping at Rhaegar's musical skills. We also know from *A Dance with Dragons* that Elia Martell, Rhaegar's wife, could not bear any more children, whilst *A Clash of Kings* tells us that Rhaegar believed his children would play an important role in preventing the return of the Others. We can infer that Rhaeger was already looking to find another wife to bear him a third child to complete the prophecy. Martin gives us most of the pieces, but it is up to the reader to put it all together, at least until the moment the truth is revealed in later volumes—if it ever is.

Wheels turn within wheels, and the information we are offered within the books is fragmentary, requiring the reader to stand back and combine the scattered facts and perspectives into a larger picture. Popular history, as spread by King Robert, tells us Lyanna was abducted and raped. Other versions of the story tell us she and Rhaegar may have been lovers, or that Rhaegar may have used her to fulfill a line in a prophecy. Even seemingly clear-cut information is not entirely trustworthy: Brandon Stark, Eddard's elder brother murdered by the Mad King, is described as a fiery but brave warrior, devoted to his betrothed, Catelyn Tully. Yet we learn in *A Dance with Dragons* that he had little to no interest in Catelyn, while another source, Ser Barristan Selmy, hints that he was a violent man. Brandon may have even sexually assaulted Ashara Dayne, getting her with child, which would explain a great deal about Ashara's pregnancy and her behavior toward the end of her life. Even what appear to be straightforward elements of backstory turn out to be more complex, more shrouded in doubt, than they first appear.

To this end, the message of A Song of Ice and Fire may be that nothing is certain, not the world's history and not the history of any individual within it. Everything is in the eye of the beholder, and the acts of one character may be heinous crimes to some but heroism to others. Tyrion Lannister tries to save King's Landing from assault by destroying Stannis Baratheon's fleet on the Blackwater. He partially succeeds—and is condemned by the people of King's Landing as a criminal and monster. The reader has a greater perspective from which to judge the characters' actions in the novels, but we are dependent on what the characters know about each other and about more ancient history. And if even contemporary events cannot be fully understood, what hope is there for the events thousands of years removed?

In *A Dance with Dragons*, we are offered a glimmer of hope, through the agency of the Last Greenseer: "[Y]ou will [. . .] see what the trees have seen," he tells Bran Stark, "be it yesterday or last year or a thousand ages past." This potentially opens up a window on the past through which Bran—and the reader—can gain a privileged vantage on events that had only been available through unreliable tales. We already have seen that the First Men used to engage in blood-sacrifices to the old gods, a truth that is not revealed in the other histories and stories. We have also seen through the heart tree that Lyanna Stark was a skilled swordswoman, capable of besting her younger brother— the future First Ranger of the Night's Watch and a very capable soldier—in mock combat. This fuels speculation that Lyanna herself was the mysterious Knight of the Laughing Tree who avenged Howland Reed's humiliation in *A Storm of Swords*, and gives another reason for why she and Rhaegar may have met and developed a connection. The addition of even a small scene, which may at first appear only to offer flavoring, can deepen our understanding of the backstory and fuel speculation.

Uncertainty as Engagement

The Song of Ice and Fire novels and the *Game of Thrones* TV series have benefited from the internet. Fans gather at blogs and online forums to debate the questions raised by each new release,

whether it's Jon Snow's parentage, the reasons for the unpredictable seasons, or the motivations of the Others. Discussions
of this sort—though sometimes very ... lively—increase the
readers' engagement with the story, allowing them the opportunity for active rather than passive participation. It helps create
and maintain a loyal and enthusiastic fanbase and gives those
fans something to talk about during the waits between novels.

As the story of A Song of Ice and Fire draws to a close, many
of the questions raised within its pages will be answered. Martin
himself has told us we will learn the reason the seasons are
out of joint and the truth behind Jon Snow's parentage. After
almost two decades of discussion, it's inevitable some fans will
have guessed those answers already, but for those who have, it's
a tribute to the skill with which the author assembled those mysteries and seeded clues to their resolutions in the story.

It's unlikely that all the mysteries will be solved, however. Larger
questions about the nature of magic and religion in the world will
surely remain, and rightfully so. Westeros itself is a place built upon
unreliable time and fractured history, so for the series to end with
mysteries still shrouding the landscape would only be fitting.

◆　◆　◆

ADAM WHITEHEAD is a British blogger resident in Britain's old-
est town and ancient Roman capital, Colchester. He is the founder
of the Wertzone blog and the *Game of Thrones* wiki. He has also
served as a moderator on the Westeros.org website since 2005. He
was nominated for the inaugural *SFX* SF Blogger of the Year Award
in 2011, for his work on the Wertzone.

◆ GARY WESTFAHL ◆

BACK TO THE EGG

The Prequels to A Song of Ice and Fire

AS ANYONE WHO EXAMINES the results can attest, a multi-volume fantasy epic requires an enormous amount of writing, and one might imagine that authors in the midst of such projects would focus their undivided attention on completing their tasks. Instead, they are often diverted into writing prequels, stories taking place before the original works begin, which may add to the depth and complexity of authors' creations but do nothing to advance the series toward the conclusion that readers are eagerly anticipating.

To be sure, the phenomenon is not limited to fantasy: in the field of science fiction, Isaac Asimov wrote his last two Foundation novels about Hari Seldon, the psychohistorian whose life predated the original trilogy, and the protagonist of

Robert A. Heinlein's final Future History novel was the mother of the series' central character, Lazarus Long. But fantasy writers seem especially prone to looking backward into their epics' prehistory: among other examples, before and after finishing The Lord of the Rings (1954–1955), J.R.R. Tolkien famously kept working on a never-completed chronicle of the events in Middle-earth that occurred long before his trilogy, assembled after his death by Christopher Tolkien as *The Silmarillion* (1977) and other works; David and Leigh Eddings wrote two prequels to their series that started with *Pawn of Prophecy* (1982); Terry Brooks has written several prequels to his original trilogy that began with *The Sword of Shannara* (1977); Robert Jordan interrupted his Wheel of Time series to produce a prequel novella, "New Spring" (1998), later expanded into a novel (2004), and intended to write other prequels before his death. And today, while writing his series A Song of Ice and Fire, George R.R. Martin has paused three times to produce novellas featuring the characters of Dunk and Egg, who lived a hundred years before the epic began, and has announced plans to write a fourth novella, assemble the existing prequels as a novel, and write additional stories about the pair. Yet readers of the series, who waited five years for its fourth installment and six years for its fifth, might well prefer that Martin focus exclusively on completing the epic's final two novels, instead of working on side projects.

Of course, it is hard to enter the minds of writers to determine precisely why they might write prequels. We know that Jordan and Martin were prodded to write their first prequels by Robert Silverberg, who solicited original novellas set in famous authors' fantasy worlds for his anthology *Legends: Short Novels by the Masters of Modern Fantasy* (1998), and that Martin's second prequel was written for Silverberg's successor volume, *Legends II: New Short Novels by the Masters of Modern Fantasy* (2004). Both writers could have fulfilled Silverberg's assignment with stories occurring in the present or future of their worlds but chose instead to venture into the past. They also continued working on prequels after Silverberg was out of the picture, suggesting sincere interest in the task. Indeed, the enigmatic first part of the dedication to *Legends II*—"For George R.R. Martin who baited the trap"—suggests that he in some fashion inspired Silverberg to edit the second anthology, perhaps to provide a venue for another Dunk and Egg story. It is also true that fantasy writers necessarily spend a great deal of time developing the prehistory of their imagined settings, and some aspect of the chore might naturally inspire a story idea deemed worth pursuing—in Martin's case, the early life of one king, Aegon V, in his Targaryen dynasty. Finally, dedicated fans often crave more information about their favorite fantasy worlds, so writers may respond by publishing prequels as a way to satisfy readers' curiosity about an imagined realm's background and history.

All of these factors might have been involved in the creation of the Dunk and Egg stories, but Martin's prequels may also demonstrate that there is something about the nature of high fantasy itself that inspires authors to keep returning to their epics' pasts instead of advancing into their futures: the main story begins to feel confining, and its past offers the possibility of freedom. Ironically, however, these prequels also suggest that such authorial efforts to temporarily escape from their own epics may ultimately prove futile.

To understand what might lead fantasy authors to write prequels, one can begin by noting that fantasy epics are usually driven by a strong sense of destiny: as a practical matter, the creators of imaginary worlds, more so than other writers, must engage in extensive planning before they begin writing, so the events they describe may project an aura of predetermination; and perhaps as a reflection of this, their characters often feel impelled to do certain things because of prophecies or prophetic signs. In the first chapter of *A Game of Thrones*, for example, Lord Eddard Stark agrees to spare a litter of dire-wolf pups when his bastard son, Jon Snow, points out that they correspond in their number and genders to his own children: "Your children were meant to have these pups, my lord." In this way, Martin immediately establishes that in his world, as in other fantasy worlds, people regard predictions and omens as important matters; further, as the epic unfolds, we learn that certain members of the Targaryen family tend to have prophetic dreams. More broadly, as in other fantasies, the major characters in the series are compelled to maintain certain loyalties, or take certain actions, solely because of the families that they were born into, or else face accusations of treason or betrayal, as various families compete for power in Westeros and beyond.

If characters feel bound to move in particular directions due to portents or family history, they may regret the loss of personal freedom but can also relish the positive outcomes that may be foretold, or that may emerge from their family connections. Yet in a still broader sense, A Song of Ice and Fire, like many fantasy series, may seem haunted by a general prediction of eventual doom. This is an argument put forth most elaborately in Northrop Frye's *Anatomy of Criticism: Four Essays* (1957), an oft-cited literary study that, in the words of the online Canadian Encyclopedia, "has had a powerful international influence on modern critical theory."

In its most influential section, covering his "Theory of Myths," Frye envisions all literature as falling within what he describes as four "*mythoi* or generic plots," corresponding to the four seasons. In this scheme, as shown in the diagram, comedy is the *mythos* of spring, which moves linearly from the dark world of experience to the bright world of innocence; romance (including fantasy) is the *mythos* of summer, which moves cyclically within the world of innocence; tragedy is the *mythos* of autumn, which moves linearly from innocence to experience; and irony and satire are the *mythos* of winter, which moves cyclically within the world of experience. Each *mythos* is further subdivided into six phases, which may shift into corresponding phases in the adjacent *mythos*, so that extended narratives can move cyclically through two or more *mythoi*. Further, while the third phase of romance, representing the quest myth that is the ancient counterpart of modern fantasy, may move on to the later phases of romance, wherein a desired outcome is successfully defended, it may also shift into the third phase of tragedy, in which heroes achieve a certain sort of triumph while also reaching a tragic end in worlds that may then descend further into the dark terrain of experience. In Frye's vision, then, the happy endings of fantasies may only be preludes to tragedies to follow, tempered solely by the hope that, after a long time, the cycle may continue turning

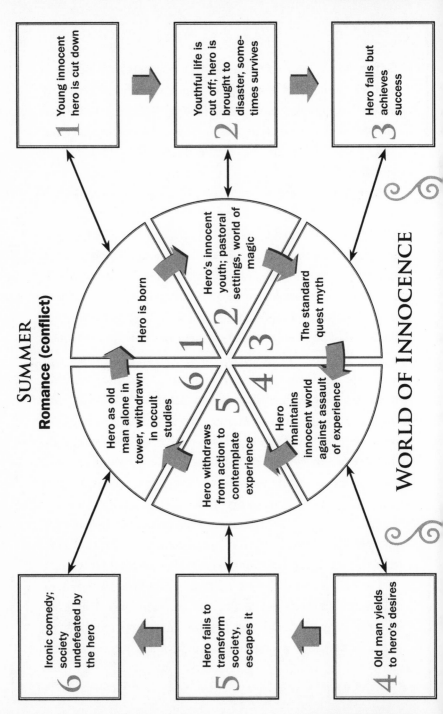

AUTUMN

SUMMER
Romance (conflict)

WORLD OF INNOCENCE

Comedy (rebirth)

1 Young innocent hero is cut down

2 Youthful life is cut off; hero is brought to disaster, sometimes survives

3 Hero falls but achieves success

Hero is born

Hero's innocent youth; pastoral settings, world of magic

The standard quest myth

Hero as old man alone in tower, withdrawn in occult studies

Hero withdraws from action to contemplate experience

Hero maintains innocent world against assault of experience

6 Ironic comedy; society undefeated by the hero

5 Hero fails to transform society, escapes it

4 Old man yields to hero's desires

1 2 3 4 5 6

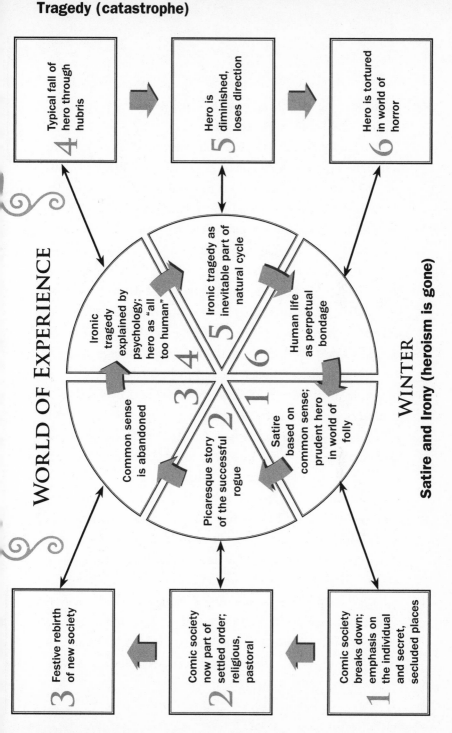

Tragedy (catastrophe)

4 Typical fall of hero through hubris

5 Hero is diminished, loses direction

6 Hero is tortured in world of horror

WORLD OF EXPERIENCE

4 Ironic tragedy explained by psychology; hero as "all too human"

5 Ironic tragedy as inevitable part of natural cycle

6 Human life as perpetual bondage

3 Common sense is abandoned

2 Picaresque story of the successful rogue

1 Satire based on common sense; prudent hero in world of folly

WINTER
Satire and Irony (heroism is gone)

SPRING

3 Festive rebirth of new society

2 Comic society now part of settled order; religious, pastoral

1 Comic society breaks down; emphasis on the individual and secret, secluded places

and the narrative will pass through irony and satire to achieve the heartening rebirth of comedy. By this argument, then, all fantasies implicitly lead to tragedies.

One hardly needs to mention that such intimations are central to the somber conclusion of The Lord of the Rings, as characters foresee the end of their magical realm and the ascendancy of the human race in the manner of the third phase of tragedy. In Martin's epic, an ominous future for his fictional world is conveyed in a literal fashion by means of seasonal imagery that Frye would understand, as the land of Westeros is entering a long, cold winter of unknown duration, and the unchallenged reign of the humans is about to be disturbed by the reappearance of the feared, frigid Others from the North. Martin has also crafted a world in which the iconic animals of fantasy, dragons, are already extinct, although the surprising births of three dragons under the control of Daenerys Targaryen provide a modicum of hope that the species may be revived. Perhaps Martin envisions a conclusion in which, all family conflicts resolved, an admirable global civilization of knights and magic is permanently forged; but considering that his saga is modeled so explicitly on Earth's medieval past, one might also anticipate that this fantasy world will eventually come to the end, to be succeeded, as in Tolkien, by a fallen world not unlike our own.

If, then, there are inevitable intimations of such dark possibilities within A Song of Ice and Fire, one alternative would be to take the story backward, into preceding phases of the cycle of romance that are related to comedy. Or, if authors resolve to explore the prehistory of their fantasy worlds for other reasons, they may find themselves naturally impelled toward stories that resemble comedy more than romance. Thus, while one can never be sure precisely what led Martin to begin writing his prequels, it is not surprising to find that, in contrast to the main epic, the resulting stories initially seem to project the lighter tone of an enjoyable diversion, reflecting the spirit of the springtime *mythos* of comedy.

The characters of Dunk and Egg, in fact, seem precisely crafted to serve as comic alternatives to the more serious-minded events of the main series. As a bastard who knows nothing about his parents, Dunk is entirely unconnected to the royal families in A Song of Ice and Fire and thus unencumbered by any inherited responsibilities. Though he impresses people with his great height, which is why he names himself "Ser Duncan the Tall," Dunk does not always seem an especially talented fighter—in the third Dunk and Egg story, "The Mystery Knight," he is easily defeated by a superior opponent. Neither does he appear to be unusually intelligent—whenever he makes a mistake, he mentally repeats what his knight used to tell him, *"Dunk the lunk, thick as a castle wall,"* and he describes Egg as *"braver than I am, and more clever."* Thus, unlike the princes and warriors of the main series, he is never burdened by high expectations as he muddles his way through an adventure. Further, by employing the accoutrements of knighthood he inherited from the knight he served as a squire, Dunk can improvise his way into the company of nobles. Yet, as a traveling "hedge knight," he can serve whatever cause or employer that seems best. Thus, he may become any sort of person he wants to be, reflecting Frye's observation that "there can hardly be such a thing as inevitable comedy," in contrast to the sense of inevitability that may, as noted, haunt the *mythos* of romance.

As for Egg, he may be of noble birth, and destined to become King Aegon V, but he has literally escaped from all the normal responsibilities of a young prince. When Dunk first encounters him, the boy has been traveling incognito (his head shaved so as not to reveal his family's distinctive golden and silvery hair), in an effort to avoid becoming his brother's squire; Dunk takes him for a stable boy and, at the youth's insistence, reluctantly employs him as his squire. Later, after his true identity is revealed, Egg insists upon remaining Dunk's squire, and when Dunk refuses to serve at court, Egg is allowed to accompany him during his travels as a knight-for-hire, still disguised as a poor boy, which Dunk indicates will serve as the best sort of training for the youthful nobleman. His nickname, in fact, has at least three meanings: of course, "Egg" is a shortened form of "Aegon"; it is an appropriate name for a bald boy, as Dunk notes— *"His head does look like an egg"*; and the egg is regularly employed as a symbol of rebirth. In a sense, Egg is being reborn, as he sheds the clothing and duties of a prince to begin learning about life from the new perspective of a common man. Indeed, when Dunk first sees Egg, he is stark naked, emerging from a bath in a stream, much like a newborn child.

It is also worth noting, in terms of seasonal imagery, that "The Hedge Knight" begins during the spring, as Dunk buries his former employer and is thus free to begin his own career as a knight, in keeping with Frye's dictum that comedy involves a transition "from a society controlled by habit, ritual bondage, arbitrary law and the older characters to a society controlled by youth and pragmatic freedom" (unlike romance, which generally focuses on the defense of an established order, not its overthrow). The introductory references to a shining sun, though interrupted by "spring rains," are pointedly dissimilar to the cold, dark night that begins *A Game of Thrones*, immediately suggesting a story with a lighter tone. The story further seems like a comedy, in its Fryean structure at least, as the lowly Dunk first bests the dissolute Prince Aerion by preventing him from harming a female puppeteer, and later defeats him in a joust, temporarily upending the social order by having a peasant triumph over a prince—a reflection of Frye's point that comedy involves "a reversal of social standards." True, the story still has significant connections to the main series: the drunken Prince Daeron provides an aura of destiny by displaying the Targaryen gift for prophetic dreams, as he relates a dream of Dunk with a dead dragon that correctly predicts the death of Prince Baelor; and since Dunk's battle with Aerion, in which each is accompanied by six knights, caused Baelor's death and led to Aerion's exile, the story contributes to the chain of improbable events that eventually placed Egg on the throne. Still, "The Hedge Knight," as a whole, seems inconsequential, as it is not a story that anyone needs to know in order to appreciate the main series.

More significantly, the story apparently sets the stage for a series of colorful adventures that will have little if any relationship to the weightier matters of A Song of Ice and Fire: Dunk and Egg will roam through the countryside, forming temporary alliances and facing various perils, with each episode contributing in some way to the maturation of Dunk and education of young Egg. This would aptly describe the second Dunk and

Egg story, "The Sworn Sword": Dunk has attached himself to a minor knight, Ser Eustace, and must take his side when a neighboring noble, the widowed Lady Rohanne, diverts his stream into her territory. Though Dunk defeats her champion in a battle, the dispute is actually settled when Lady Rohanne, who needs a husband to legally keep her land, unexpectedly agrees to marry Ser Eustace. In the meantime, having discovered that Ser Eustace fought for would-be usurper Daemon in the Blackfyre Rebellion, a disillusioned Dunk resolves to leave his service and seek another assignment.

Overall, the story matches the pattern of Frye's *mythos* of comedy, not the quest myth of romance. First, while a devastating draught does provide a dramatic background for the story, an effort to get one's opponents to dismantle a dam necessarily seems less grand than the conflicts typically observed in fantasy; at one point, Dunk dismisses the matter as "just some pissing contest." Dunk's brief efforts to train some of Ser Eustace's peasants for a possible battle reveal that the men are comically inept, and when Dunk refuses to let Egg accompany him to a confrontation with Lady Rohanne, the boy goes behind his back to persuade Ser Eustace to require his presence, leading Dunk to ruefully lament that he had been *"Outwitted by a boy of ten,"* reinforcing the idea that he is none too bright. While Dunk does win his concluding battle, it is a clumsy affair, taking place in a stream and utterly lacking the dignity of a knightly joust. In addition, the battle turns out to be of little import, as matters are actually resolved by an unexpected and incongruous marriage, which Frye describes as the "most common" conclusion for a comedy. The marriage also represents an example of the sorts of "manipulation" and "unlikely conversions" that typically occur at the end of comedies.

Still, despite its generally comic spirit, some aspects of "The Sworn Sword" suggest a shift toward the more somber world of romance. First, while the literal seasons of stories may not always correspond to their metaphorical seasons (according to Frye's theory), it may be significant that this tale is set in summer, not in spring, and the more portentous matters of dynastic succession again intrude upon the diversion, as Ser Eustace's old involvement in the effort to oust King Daeron II becomes a key element in the plot. In addition, Ser Eustace is portrayed as a man who is living in the past, constantly telling stories about battles that occurred long ago and recalling his family's formerly elevated status; as his knight Ser Bennis dismissively notes, the man keeps talking "about how great he used to be." In contrast to comedy, his attitude seems to reflect the "extraordinarily persistent nostalgia" that Frye sees as characteristic of romance, and Ser Eustace further illustrates that such inclinations can be harmful: obsessed with memories of happier days, Ser Eustace has neglected to maintain any forces that could credibly fight on his behalf, so that Dunk feels compelled to drive away the poorly prepared peasants he hastily recruited for the task, making it likely that the knight will permanently lose the stream that is vital to his estate.

In the end, though, Ser Eustace recovers by forcefully stepping into the present, accepting Lady Rohanne's point that "The world changes," and, by marrying her, he forges an improbable alliance that serves both of their interests. Intriguingly, one might interpret this development as a coded message to the authors of prequels: stop obsessing over the past of your imagined worlds and get back to their present. Without interviewing Martin, of course, one cannot tell if any such meaning was intended, or if he was in fact getting feedback from fans who were growing impatient with his prequels. Still, if an author ever feels the need to defend the creation of prequels, there are two possible approaches: to simply assert that, as a matter of responsibility, an author who starts writing prequels, for whatever reason, should finish their story; or to resolve to make the prequels seem more portentous, more integral to the main series, so they cannot be attacked as frivolous diversions.

Interestingly, there is evidence in the third novel of A Song of Ice and Fire, *A Storm of Swords*, suggesting precisely such a desire to heighten the import of the Dunk and Egg stories. In one scene, Jaime Lannister, the new Lord Commander of the Kingsguard, mentions Dunk as one of his distinguished predecessors:

> The chair behind the table was old black oak, with cushions of blanched cowhide, the leather worn thin. *Worn by the bony arse of Barristan the Bold and Ser Gerold Hightower before him, by Prince Aemon the Dragonknight, Ser Ryam Redwyne, and the Demon of Darry, by Ser Duncan the Tall and the Pale Griffin Alyn Connington.* How could the Kingslayer belong in such exalted company?

He also reads a biography of Barristan that mentions, as one of his noteworthy deeds, that he bested Ser Duncan at a tournament. And in case readers did not recall these fleeting references,

Martin reminds them of Dunk's fate throughout the third Dunk and Egg story, "The Mystery Knight": Ser John the Fiddler, later revealed to be the son of the rebel Daemon Blackfyre, prophetically dreams that Dunk will become "a Sworn Brother of the Kingsguard," though Dunk ironically ridicules the idea on three occasions.

A man originally presented as a humble commoner, then, has been recast as someone, like Egg, who is destined to become a renowned figure, and he could hardly advance to such an elevated status by continuing to engage in petty squabbles involving rustic nobles. Instead, to explain his fate, Martin must provide him with adventures that will function in some way to elevate his stature, just as T.H. White elevated the stature of Arthur in moving from *The Sword in the Stone* (1938) to the later novels in The Once and Future King tetralogy (1938–1958), and as Tolkien elevated the stature of hobbits in moving from *The Hobbit* (1937) to The Lord of the Rings. This would provide one explanation for the tonal shift observed in "The Mystery Knight." Ostensibly, this will simply be another random adventure for the pair, as Dunk and Egg, while traveling north to seek employment, encounter some knights who inform them about an upcoming wedding where there will be a joust, and Dunk decides to participate in the tournament.

However, this is also another story that takes place in the summer, not the spring, as the story opens with Dunk and Egg riding through a "light summer rain," and the tournament turns out to be far more significant than Dunk and Egg suspect. For Daemon's disguised son and other compatriots are actually gathering at the wedding to launch a second rebellion against

King Daeron II, as Egg comes to suspect when he notices that many of its participants were involved in the first revolt. Further, after providing some inadvertent assistance in thwarting this effort, Dunk gets to meet the King's Hand himself, the powerful Bloodraven, who thus becomes personally aware of the knight who has been secretly training his princely relative. So, having helped to prevent a rebellion, and having made a friend in high places, Dunk now seems better positioned for his eventual elevation to the Kingsguard, though further triumphs will presumably be necessary before he achieves that status.

As a small but significant sign of how the stories are changing, Bloodraven had previously figured as an unseen but constantly dreaded presence, said to be a sorcerer with spies everywhere, listening for the first signs of treasonous activity; in "The Sworn Sword," recalling the time he had seen the man, Dunk reports that "the memory made him shiver," and he regularly repeats a paranoid joke suggesting his pervasive vigilance: "*How many eyes does Lord Bloodraven have?* [...] *A thousand eyes, and one.*" This is exactly what typical characters in comedy, members of the lower class like Dunk, would think about a powerful and oppressive ruler. Yet at the end of "The Mystery Knight," Bloodraven has a conversation with Dunk in which he comes across as a harsh but reasonable ruler, even capable of laughing at the imprudent demands of his cousin Egg, and Egg implicitly defends his ruthlessness by recalling what the man had told his father, that "it was better to be frightening than frightened." Suddenly, Bloodraven seems a more likable fellow, perfectly in keeping with the main series' theme of unreliable perspectives and tales; and the man who once feared him, and felt "ill-at-ease" around nobles in "The Hedge Knight," has now spoken to him almost as an equal, signaling that Dunk has entered the company of royals and will henceforth share their attitudes.

And, while one can never be certain where Martin's future prequels will take their characters, it would be reasonable to anticipate that later stories, like "The Mystery Knight," will have Dunk, accompanied by a maturing Egg, continue to mingle with the royal names on the Westerosi genealogy charts, bolster his reputation by means of significant accomplishments, and eventually earn promotion to the Kingsguard, one of the highest posts available to a person not of royal blood. One might also speculate that his feats will prove to be important precursors to certain developments in the main series, to answer any possible objections to Martin's ongoing attention to the character. As another aspect of Dunk's growing prominence, it is also possible that Martin will clear up the mystery of his birth, perhaps revealing that he is in fact related to one of the epic's great families. Indeed, Dunk's vivid dreams, his concession to Ser John that he had also prophetically dreamed of joining the Kingsguard, and his earlier comment that "We'd all be bastard sons of old King Aegon if half these tales were true," serve as hints that he is part of the Targaryen family.

In taking such steps, Martin would effectively transform the Dunk and Egg stories into essential precursors to A Song of Ice and Fire, and in the future, perhaps, one or more volumes of Dunk and Egg stories, not *A Game of Thrones*, will be presented as the true beginning of the series. And we see that the expectations raised by the end of the first Dunk and Egg tale—of a series of engaging but inconsequential adventures involving

an itinerant knight and his squire—are not being met, and that
these stories are instead taking on an aura of dignity and significance that recalls the original series, as they now involve the
heroic achievements of a future military leader and the education of a future king.

It thus becomes necessary to modify the hypothesis previously advanced about the writing of prequels: it may *appear* that
prequels would offer opportunities to craft comedic companion pieces to more portentous epics, but the resulting prequels
inexorably come to replicate the nature and atmosphere of the
original stories, becoming, one might say, portentous epics in
themselves. Certainly, whatever escape Tolkien might have
sought in his own inchoate prequels to The Lord of the Rings
was never achieved, as all the materials in *The Silmarillion* mimic
the grandeur of their predecessors. In the form of the detailed
material eventually assembled as *The Children of Húrin* (2007),
they even took on an explicitly tragic tone never observed in the
trilogy itself. It is similarly possible that the Dunk and Egg stories, as their protagonists assume their royal roles and advance
toward their already-chronicled deaths, will start to project the
sense of impending tragedy arguably implicit in the original
series. It might even become necessary to begin describing these
prequels as the Duncan and Aegon stories, not the Dunk and
Egg stories, to better reflect their burgeoning *gravitas*.

Thus, instead of providing Martin with alternative, lighter
works to accompany the more serious main components of
A Song of Ice and Fire series, the Dunk and Egg stories have
become a serious matter in themselves, a second important task
that Martin must complete, in addition to the original epic.

Now, with two similar assignments in his inbox, whatever originally led Martin to begin writing prequels may now inspire him to launch another series of prequels involving new characters, which would again offer the possibility of diverting, comedic adventures. And if this begins to seem like an endless circular pattern, it would represent another variation on the cyclical narratives that Northrop Frye has argued are central to all forms of fantasy.

◆ ◆ ◆

GARY WESTFAHL, now retired from the University of California, Riverside, works as an Adjunct Professor at the University of La Verne. In addition to publishing hundreds of articles and reviews, including over fifty film reviews for Locus Online, he is the author, editor, or co-editor of over twenty books about science fiction and fantasy, including the Hugo Award–nominated *Science Fiction Quotations: From the Inner Mind to the Outer Limits* and *The Greenwood Encyclopedia of Science Fiction and Fantasy: Themes, Works, and Wonders*. In 2003, he won the Science Fiction Research Association's Pilgrim Award for his lifetime contributions to science fiction and fantasy scholarship.

ART IMITATES WAR

Post-Traumatic Stress Disorder in
A Song of Ice and Fire

IT'S HARD TO ZERO in on what makes A Song of Ice and Fire so incredibly compelling. It's one of the most celebrated and famous works in modern fantasy, on par with Tolkien, Jordan, or Sanderson. If there's one specific area I like to hone in on, it's Martin's facility with character. Martin routinely steps into the mindsets of a wide range of characters who are nothing like him. We see through the eyes of Cersei, a haughty woman; Tyrion, a crippled dwarf; Bran, a broken little boy; Petyr Baelish, a politically connected schemer. The list goes on: eunuchs, mothers, blacksmiths, bastards, even animals and monsters. Each one fully realized. Each one authentic.

And each one suffering from intense trauma. Martin's not very nice to his characters. Westeros is a rough place to grow up.

Every single major character in the saga is horribly traumatized at some point, and that trauma is exacerbated as their stories evolve. It's in that trauma, and how his characters react to it, that I see Martin at his best.

I've been to war three times and responded to two major domestic disasters. I've seen what serious mental and emotional trauma does to people firsthand. I never expected that experience to apply to a work of fantasy. But by the time I finished *A Dance with Dragons*, I realized with a start that Martin had captured the range of reactions associated with Post-Traumatic Stress Disorder (PTSD). More surprising, Martin was portraying PTSD accurately, as it *really* happens, rather than the common misconceptions of the condition. Martin's realization of traumatized characters dazzled me with its authenticity. He got an essential and often missed aspect of PTSD exactly right: sometimes traumatic experiences profoundly damage a character, but sometimes they enfranchise and strengthen the sufferer. These polar opposite, yet fully authentic PTSD reactions, are exhibited in A Song of Ice and Fire through two major characters: Arya Stark, enfranchised as a result of trauma, and Theon Greyjoy, destroyed by it.

Now, I should add a caveat here. I'm not a trained mental health professional. I'm a guy with some experiences as to how PTSD manifests. Experts might bridle at my interpretations, but the study and definition of PTSD is a new frontier in mental health. The phenomenon changes as the nature of battle and the warrior-lifestyle changes, and the speed of that change is faster than ever before. As of just a couple of months ago, military suicide rates were at an all-time high in the United States. In moving to help those who suffer from PTSD, we are building the plane as it flies.

To understand how this discussion applies to the characters, one has to understand what PTSD is and how it functions. It's currently dealt with as an almost physical pathology. You're examined, you're diagnosed, you're prescribed a course of treatment. You take home leave or bed rest. You respond to your meds or your course of therapy, and you go back to work, right as rain, as if you'd gotten over a patch of strep throat. Though a hat is tipped to the chronic nature of the condition, the emphasis remains on it as pathology.

PTSD and the Cooper Color System

But PTSD is far more insidious and enduring. To understand how it impacts victims, we are best guided by the color code created by Jeff Cooper, a US Marine and firearms instructor. His color system, originally intended to develop a "combat mindset" that would enable people to survive sudden, lethal confrontation, was first laid out in his book *Principles of Personal Defense* (1989) and later adapted in the seminal work by Ed Lovette and Dave Spaulding, *Defensive Living* (2000), which I, like many folks bound for Iraq and Afghanistan, read as part of my predeployment training.

The Cooper Color Code posits that most individuals, at least in relatively safe, peaceful societies as in the US and Europe, live in "Condition White." They are blissfully unaware of danger. When a sudden exposure to trauma occurs, most people in Condition White will shift immediately into "Condition

Black," a defenseless posture of frozen panic or denial. People in Condition Black will often behave in self-destructive fashion, surrendering to attackers who clearly have no intention to take prisoners, retreating into disbelief ("this can't be happening to me"), or simply going catatonic.

Cooper argued that Condition Black could best be avoided by training those in combat situations to live always in "Condition Yellow," a relaxed but vigilant state where an individual maintains constant situational awareness. In Iraq, we called it "having your head on a swivel." An individual in Condition Yellow is constantly thinking, *I may have to fight at any moment*, and is prepared to do so.

Here's where PTSD is particularly nasty. It isn't really a "disorder" as modern medical experts understand it. It's a shift in perspective. Being forced into Condition Black *and* being trained to live in Condition Yellow are both highly traumatizing. *Both* shift your worldview, often permanently. Both become hard-coded into personality, changing the individual in ways they never expected. Sometimes, amazingly enough, for the better.

But still, traumatizing. It's easy for people to understand the Condition Black shift—an individual forever frightened of the world, seeing the veil ripped away and the horror of mortality revealed in all its stark reality. Such individuals manifest aspects of Condition Black throughout their peacetime lives. They are frozen, frightened, numb. They can be catatonic, either naturally or through the anesthetizing use of drugs and alcohol. The self-destructive behaviors of Condition Black can also manifest in coping mechanisms after the trauma has passed. Sufferers may lash out at friends and family, engage in addictive behavior, sink in a mire of self-pity. Cooper discusses Condition Black in terms of its immediate impact in a combat situation, but it has enduring effects as a part of PTSD and how those who have experienced trauma deal with the aftermath throughout their lives.

The same is true for those living in Condition Yellow. It, too, is a coping mechanism that endures long past the initial trauma. I cannot walk down a street without wondering who is behind me, who is around each corner I pass. I can't sit comfortably in a restaurant or café unless I am facing the entrance, my back to a wall. My hands automatically fly to my "workspace"—in front of my face where I can see my pistol slide to work the action—whenever I hear a car backfire. I check locks and alarms obsessively. A homeless man grasped my elbow from behind once to get my attention. I almost flattened him. Some would say these effects are minor. I assure you they're not. Constant heightened vigilance is absolutely exhausting, physically and mentally. Over the years, it digs grooves in you.

With such a shift in perspective, a personal holocaust usually ensues, as the PTSD sufferer's pre-trauma worldview is revealed to be false. Illusions of security, which often form the bedrock of people's daily lives, are ripped away. Most of us are able to work and play without thinking about what threats loom all around us, about how quickly and cheaply our lives can be snuffed out. With the realization of the immediacy of threats, the basis on which we construct our lives is razed.

And what is razed must be reassembled.

Here is where PTSD can enfranchise as well as cripple. A host of factors play into how the PTSD sufferer constructs a new life. Many permanently shift into Condition Black, rebuilding on a foundation of horror and withering fear. Others, and I'd argue fewer, move into Condition Yellow, scarred, but equipped to face future traumatic events. PTSD sufferers often slide on a scale between the two extremes of Conditions Yellow and Black, sometimes oscillating between them day by day. But for the purposes of illustrating their manifestation in Martin's epic, extremes are helpful.

Arya Stark and Condition Yellow

"Needle was Winterfell's grey walls, and the laughter of its people."

—*A Feast for Crows*

While Condition Yellow is still a traumatized state, it is an enfranchised one. Those who react to trauma by moving into Condition Yellow engage what some would consider positive coping mechanisms, such as hypervigilance, coldhearted decision-making, rapid reactions to dangerous situations, extra attention to personal safety, commitment to training and lifestyle decisions that ensure readiness for future traumatic events.

I don't want to understate that these are coping mechanisms. A person in permanent Condition Yellow is traumatized and suffering from PTSD. It's not usually a happy place to be, but in terms of external perception, it is one that is more likely to ensure the "success" of the sufferer in terms of their long-term survival.

Arya Stark, like so many in war, is yanked from relative security while still a child. Raised as the scion of a noble house, one of the most privileged positions a person can enjoy in the brutal world of Westeros, she witnesses her first horrible murder at the tender age of nine. It is the slaughter of the peasant boy Mycah, whom she defended against Prince Joffrey's torments. The death goes hand in hand with the loss of one of the family's precious direwolves and Arya's separation from her own wolf, Nymeria. Perhaps most significantly, it is casual, unjust violence perpetrated by an enemy with power but little conscience. Mycah and Lady are killed almost as an afterthought, with nearly no effort being made to do what is just in the presence of the overwhelming power of the Iron Throne.

That is precisely the sort of veil-rending experience that can bring about the shift in worldview so common in those who suffer from PTSD. A little girl, raised with illusions of justice and safety, must suddenly confront the reality of her world. Those in power, often with a thoughtless flick of the wrist, can destroy those things we hold most dear. It isn't long before trauma builds on trauma, as Arya witnesses the destruction of her family and the brutal execution of her father. Yoren may cover her eyes, but she knows what is happening.

But Arya is the daughter of Ned Stark, raised by men-of-war who have been in Condition Yellow since the Battle of the Trident and almost certainly much earlier. When Arya resists the role of court lady that her sister Sansa so readily accepts, the men of her family respond with surprising adaptability. They bring her, reluctantly and as gently as they can, into their warrior world.

The gifting of Needle and her training by the Braavosi fencer Syrio Forel are perhaps the most symbolic of Arya's entry into Condition Yellow. While the wages of war are not yet fully upon her, she is being slowly hardened to a dangerous world. The physical instruments of combat are real, tangible coping devices. Arya will later come to rely on her internal strength, but initially, the sword and the training to use it represent the budding seeds of her new outlook on life. Arya best displays her commitment to Condition Yellow and her departure from the traditional female role in her world in the scene where Jon Snow reminds her that the best swords all have names. "Sansa can keep her sewing needles," Arya replies, in her television incarnation. "I have a Needle of my own" ("The Kingsroad").

The razing of worldview and reconstruction of perspective happen quite literally for Arya. She reacts to her trauma by abandoning her identity and reinventing herself from the roots up no less than ten times, assuming identities ranging from her wolf Nymeria, into whose skin she can slip, to Arry, an orphan boy and street urchin, to Beth, the blind beggar who ultimately carries out her first assassination for the Faceless Men. In this case, the measure is also practical, as she is the heir of a noble house, easily recognized and relentlessly hunted.

Arya's trauma rips her world away. Cast out on the streets of Flea Bottom, she recreates herself as capable, warlike, alert. Surrounded by death, she dedicates herself to its study; murdering, impulsively at first with the King's Landing stable boy, then deliberately and with decreasing difficulty, first through Jaqen H'ghar, and later by her own hands and Nymeria's teeth. Her *raison d'etre*, which had once been balancing her adventurous ways with the traditions of her home and family, is replaced by her chanted prayer: the list of names of the victims she swears to avenge herself upon: "'Ser Gregor,' she'd whisper to her stone pillow. [. . .] 'Ser Amory, Ser Ilyn, Ser Meryn, King Joffrey, Queen Cersei.'" (*A Clash of Kings*).

Arya emerges from the crucible of her trauma horribly changed. Even by the harsh standards of Westeros, her childhood has been ripped away. She is shaken to her roots.

Still, the coping mechanisms she develops to grapple with PTSD *strengthen* her. She is more capable and powerful than she was before the incidents that transformed her. By the close of *A Dance with Dragons*, she is well on the path of establishing herself as a dedicated and able professional assassin: street-smart, intuitive, remorseless, and deadly.

Condition Yellow has become integrated into Arya's character. She is enfranchised: no less traumatized for the transformation, but no weaker either.

Theon Greyjoy and Condition Black

"Only a fool humbles himself when the world is so full of men eager to do that job for him."

—A CLASH OF KINGS

Those in Condition Black generally engage coping mechanisms that most external viewers would perceive as negative. Those who move into permanent Condition Black as a result of PTSD are actively self-destructive, usually in one of two ways. Some freeze up, go catatonic, and fail to react to future traumatic events, essentially letting the world have its way with them. Alternately, those in Condition Black may actively engage in self-destruction through means of compulsive behavior such as drug, alcohol, or sex addiction. Detached from a world that has come to terrify them, they may engage in suicidal levels of risk-taking or push away loved ones who try to help.

Theon Greyjoy, on the surface, has a similar upbringing to Arya's, with its attached illusions of safety. But there is one key difference: Theon lives as a hostage—but ostensibly a member— of the Stark family in exchange for the good behavior of his own kinsmen, the Greyjoys of the Iron Isles.

While Arya is coaxed into Condition Yellow by a wary and loving family, Theon is ripped from his warlike kin and thrust into a setting that is soft by comparison. The Starks are certainly warlike, but life in Winterfell is a far cry from life on the Iron Isles, where every aspect of existence from birth on is imbued with the trappings of war. Yet Theon is mistrusted by the people who hold him hostage. He is given no succor, no gentle coaxing into preparedness against the slings and arrows of life. He lacks the cushion of a gift like Needle and a patient and gentle fencing master. For Theon, the slide to Condition Black begins early.

Theon's life in Winterfell is framed by constant reminders that he lives at the mercy of his captors, contingent upon the good behavior of his own clan. He is treated even worse than the bastard Jon Snow, who lacks even his noble blood. Robb Stark reinforces his outcast status after Theon bravely saves Bran's life. "Jon always said you were an ass, Greyjoy," Robb says of Theon's decision to use his bow to fell Bran's assailant, even though the shot was perfect and the boy was unharmed. "I ought to chain

you up in the yard and let Bran take a few practice shots at *you*"
(*A Game of Thrones*).

The signs of Condition Black manifest early in Theon's narrative. Many who suffer from PTSD engage in addictive, self-
destructive behavior. Martin represents this with sex, in Greyjoy's
case, painting him as a whoremonger of some renown. Like an
addict, Greyjoy uses sex not so much as a source of pleasure but
to assuage a compulsion. He recalls tumbling the miller's wife
"a time or two" in *A Clash of Kings* and that there was "nothing
special" about her, displaying a lack of satisfaction in the act.
Sex also appears to be a way for Theon to grasp some shred of
personal power when, as a hostage, so much has been stripped
from him. This is reflected in the adulterous nature of some of
Theon's conquests, and in the way he takes pleasure in demean-
ing his former paramours, such as Kyra. After embarrassing her
publicly, he confides to Robb Stark, "She squirms like a weasel
in bed, but say a word to her on the street, and she blushes pink
as a maid" (*A Game of Thrones*). He then tries to launch into a
detailed tale of a sexual encounter before Robb cuts him off.

The self-destructive nature of Greyjoy's sex addiction is further expanded on when his sister Asha seduces him as a means
to humiliate him. When Theon is sent on embassy to his former
home, he doesn't recognize his sister, and so attempts to court
her. Asha, who recognizes Theon and his weakness, plays along
and only later reveals herself as his sister. Her deceit is also the
final blow in a string of rejections by his own family, rebuffs that
leave him utterly adrift: his Ironborn kin declare him soft and
weak from too many years in Winterfell. They despise him. The
Starks, in turn, have shown they will never fully trust him and

are all too willing to use him for their own political ends. Ned Stark reminds readers of this when he warns his wife that a close watch be kept on Theon because, "If there is war, we shall have sore need of his father's fleet" (*A Game of Thrones*). The goal is not to keep him safe, but to keep him secure as a bargaining chip.

After his rejection by his biological family, Greyjoy's self-destructive impulses spill their banks. Some may argue that Theon's seizure of Winterfell is the bold action of a man intent on standing alone and proving his worth to a family that judges men by their feats of arms. I see it more as the spiteful lashing out of a child wounded by everyone around him, all those he loves and might love. This is classic Condition Black: Theon engages in highly risky behavior, flailing in reaction to trauma he cannot handle. Arya's choices are deliberate, empowered. Theon's are reactive, driven by his inability to reconcile the real world with the one he thought he'd lived in.

Theon mostly vanishes from *A Storm of Swords* and *A Feast for Crows*, though there are some hints as to what may become of him when a piece of his skin is delivered to Catelyn Stark at the Red Wedding. This gruesome token is an indication of what is occurring offstage: Theon's shift into Condition Black becoming permanent under the continuous torture he is suffering at the hands of Ramsay Bolton. When Theon reappears in *A Dance with Dragons*, his transformation is complete.

Like Arya, Theon has abandoned his old identity and reconstructed himself fully, though in his case, in a Condition Black identity, not a Condition Yellow one. Where Arya becomes a capable, savvy, and adaptive fighter, Theon sinks fully into self-pity, terror, and paralysis. He emerges from this morass as the stinking, haunted Reek, lickspittle and lackey to his torturer, the monster Ramsay, the Bastard of Bolton. When we are first introduced to Reek in *A Dance with Dragons*, he has fallen so low that he is eating rats. As the guards approach his cell, his only thought is: *"If they catch me with it, they will take it away, and then they'll tell, and Lord Ramsay will hurt me."*

Where Arya's litany is one of empowerment—a hit list of her enemies—Theon's is a reminder to adhere to a path of self-destruction: *"Serve and obey and remember your name. Reek, Reek, it rhymes with meek"* (*A Dance with Dragons*). Arya faces each new enemy and trauma with renewed determination. Through the chaos in the Red Keep, life on the streets of Flea Bottom, the rigors of Harrenhal, she continuously remakes herself to best face her current challenges and to prepare for the next. Theon has the opposite reaction to the flaying, the loss of his teeth, the false hope engendered by his escape from the Dreadfort and the horror of the subsequent hunt he endures, and the destruction of his former lover Kyra. Each blow leveled against him lowers him further into the identity of Reek.

Again, some may sympathize, arguing that the torture Theon endures would undo any man. Theon is broken physically to an extent from which he can never recover, subjected to agonies that would snap the strongest spines.

Few could stand up to torture of the kind Bolton inflicts upon Theon, and it leaves him with a grim choice between death or the loss of his identity. Condition Black becomes the framework he embraces to cling to life. I have met many service members returned from Iraq and Afghanistan missing limbs. One friend had been "double-tapped": hit by an improvised explosive timed to detonate slightly after a primary charge, in a deliberate effort to strike at first responders to a blast. He is a jigsaw puzzle, his face and body crisscrossed with black lines. One eye is gone, his arm missing below the elbow. But his identity remains unscathed. The breaking of his body, the constant agony, the bitterness over the unfairness of the trauma he has suffered— these things have not touched the man he is inside. Theon's reaction to torture and trauma may be the more likely outcome, but it is not the only possible one. There are men who would die before allowing themselves to become Reek, no matter what was done to them.

The Reek identity is the best example of a permanent Condition Black that I have ever encountered in fiction. The chilling scene where Ramsay forces Theon to abase himself and the false "Arya," Jeyne Poole, embodies the depredations life in that bleak zone can subject a person to. It is the ultimate and most horrifying outcome of PTSD, the fate of a person utterly incapable of coping with the trauma he faces.

Theon Greyjoy's plight nearly brought me to tears, because I have seen that transformation before, every bit as total and harrowing, until death seems a mercy in comparison.

Getting It Right

Post-Traumatic Stress Disorder has been around for as long as mankind has experienced trauma, but the wars in Iraq and Afghanistan are only now forcing it on to the national stage as a mental health issue requiring serious attention. As with all new fields of study, the initial attempts to define the parameters of the problem—to discover predictable, repeating, and therefore treatable behaviors and symptoms—are a lot of fumbling in the dark. Complex issues defy taxonomy. Things work a certain way, except when they don't. The human mind is an incredibly intricate mechanism.

The Cooper Color Code is a limited, and perhaps even woefully inadequate, way to categorize reactions to trauma. It is designed to deal with immediate, rapidly evolving tactical situations. Yet it provides us with a surprisingly pertinent means to frame the problem of long-term PTSD. It becomes another tool we can use to discuss the issue, to start sketching out the parameters we must understand if we're ever going to begin finding solutions. The Cooper Color Code is an analogy, a way of saying, "PTSD is like this."

Ironically, fiction, in this case fantasy, becomes another tool in that toolbox, as Martin's epic saga and his characters' actions within it provide us with another analogy we can use to try to define coping mechanisms, to identify them as associated with response to trauma, and to begin to address the problems they present. The behaviors of Arya and Theon, as well as other characters in A Song of Ice and Fire, so closely reflect behaviors I have seen in real combatants returning from war, in real crisis responders dealing with the aftermath of their experiences, that it shouldn't go unremarked. In this, Martin's facility with character may be a useful and even powerful new angle from which to approach the problem, and his writing a window into the plight of those struggling in the shadow of PTSD.

◆ ◆ ◆

MYKE COLE is the author of the military fantasy Shadow Ops series, the first novel of which, *Control Point*, is currently available from Ace. As a security contractor, government civilian and military officer, Myke Cole's career has run the gamut from counterterrorism to cyber warfare to federal law enforcement. He's done three tours in Iraq and was recalled to serve during the Deepwater Horizon oil spill. He also served as a Hurricane Duty Officer (HDO) during Hurricane Irene.

◆ SUSAN VAUGHT ◆

THE BRUTAL COST OF REDEMPTION IN WESTEROS

Or, What *Moral Ambiguity?*

IN HIS ESSAY "EPIC Pooh," Michael Moorcock postulates that J.R.R. Tolkien's Lord of the Rings trilogy barely rises above nursery-room prose that "tells you comforting lies." Moorcock describes the epic as an anti-romance, laced with the author's Christian belief system to the point that faith is substituted for artistic rigor. Tolkien's peasants serve as a "bulwark against Chaos [. . .]. They don't ask any questions of white men in grey clothing who somehow have a handle on what's best for us." James L. Sutter furthers this idea in his November 2011 guest essay at Suvudu entitled "The Gray Zone: Moral Ambiguity in Fantasy," noting that The Lord of the Rings has a fairy-tale simplicity, drawing on good and evil archetypes so stark that all the characters can easily be sorted into the boring categories of obviously "good" or irre-futably "bad."

Sutter raises George R.R. Martin's A Song of Ice and Fire as a contrast, proclaiming that Martin demonstrates one antidote to the boring good/evil clarity of Tolkien, which is to "remove the boundaries altogether [. . .]. Few of his characters are unimpeach-ably good or irredeemably evil." This description is right in line with those offered by other commentators. Heather Havrilesky, in her 2011 New York Times review of the HBO adaptation of Martin's epic, terms the tale "hedonistic and bleak," and hints that it embodies a nihilistic worldview. Sutter goes even further. He notes that the series has a "lack of moralistic signposts." Like many readers and critics, he identifies the world of Westeros as a place best described as morally ambiguous.

This perception appears to arise from the fact that charac-ters cannot easily be sorted into fixed categories of "good" or "evil" based on intentions, character traits, actions, alliances, or outcomes. Unlike the archetypal heroes and villains in Tolkien's work, characters in Westeros are often damaged, flawed, and beset by overwhelming emotions or passions that twist their heroic intent. Outcomes seem to reward bad behavior and cor-rupt intentions, and to punish good behavior and even the purest of intentions. The linear high-fantasy path of do-good-and-win (after some frightening setbacks)/do-evil-and-fall (after a few seemingly large victories) is not present in Westeros. Characters are often without clear alignments, and even if they manage to align with seemingly good or evil poles, this does little to ensure success, failure, or even survival. Even more importantly, we have no single, omniscient, reliable narrator to count on for guidance in this shadowy landscape. Readers see the action in Westeros exclusively through the fragmented, contradictory perspectives of its inhabitants. Much as in real life, we relate to some of the point-of-view characters and find little in common with others. We love some, we hate some, and through the filters of our own emotional, cognitive, and social biases, we do not always do well judging whether or not they represent good or evil by the standards of the Seven Kingdoms.

And there *are* standards.

To the observations and criticisms citing the lack of clear definitions of good and evil, I say: *What* moral ambiguity?

The Ways of the World

Westeros is not built upon a shifting foundation of chaos. True, there is no clearly marked, brightly lit path to salvation. Yet characters face a painful retributive justice, born of moral absolutism, that lends reality and depth to the medieval society portrayed in the series.

To grasp the cosmology at play in Westeros, consideration must be given to the way its society defines sin and evil. Since there is no distant, satanic eye atop a tower spawning unthinking mobs of obviously violent minions, evil must have a more mundane manifestation, and that manifestation arises from the fundamental threat to existence in the Seven Kingdoms: interminable winter—*Winter*—and the creatures Winter brings. "Winter Is Coming" becomes a denotative and connotative statement of the society's core value and needs. In a very literal sense, the words of the Stark motto are a reminder that Winter will come to Westeros, as it always has, and it will bring with it terror and death that transcend typical human experiences. The more subtle shadings of the statement imply that for society to survive, residents of Westeros must keep to older traditions of working together in peace, productivity, and respect, to plan for this devastation. Otherwise, they will all perish when the light vanishes, the snow starts to fall, and the dead things begin to shuffle and stomp across the countryside.

Characters who engage in murder, sadistic cruelty, malignant selfishness or narcissism, dishonorable and dishonest acts, and obsessions with relative frivolities such as political intrigue and playing the game of thrones transgress against not just individuals but society itself. Those who fail to understand that Winter is coming—who fail to recognize that they must put aside lesser concerns and any bad behavior that gets in the way of preserving the kingdom—represent evil in Westeros. They commit sins against the unity necessary to survive the coming darkness, either to such a level that they become irredeemable, or to lesser extents, with failure or refusal to comprehend the seriousness of their wrongdoings. There is no ambiguity in the fate of characters who cannot or will not choose a path of redemption. They suffer, and they die, often in a fashion that approaches ironic justice. Robb Stark, Catelyn Stark, and Joffrey Baratheon serve as examples of characters who face this fate.

In Westeros, as in the real world, there are few if any saints, or even adults, who do not sin at one level of severity or another. Only the very young seem to have claim to complete innocence and impunity. Those who violate the moral and actual laws of the land, but grasp the depth of their indiscretions and attempt to atone—those who seem to truly understand that Winter *is* coming, and everything that the words imply—serve as representatives of good in Westeros. These characters still walk a wicked road of atonement that can be staggering. There is no ambiguity for them, either. They will suffer. They will lose everything and be reduced to nothing, and they will have to find the strength to rebuild their identities, or die along the way and be heartlessly forgotten. Davos Seaworth, Sansa Stark, and Jaime Lannister appear to be struggling through such grueling journeys of redemption.

The Winter Path

Robb Stark, the young and newly proclaimed King in the North, does good in Westeros by establishing a measure of peace and unity amongst disparate groups when he gives his word that he will marry a daughter of Lord Walder Frey. He then breaks that promise by marrying his nursemaid, Jeyne Westerling. His reasons for marrying Jeyne are honorable, as he is attempting to protect her reputation after he takes her maidenhead; however, these reasons apply primarily to individual needs, namely Jeyne's need for this protection and Robb's need to avoid the guilt related to his sin of lust and how it might affect Jeyne in the future. As a citizen of Westeros, and especially as a man purporting to be a king, Robb fails to recognize the magnitude of his more serious sins: the tarnishing of his honor through his oathbreaking not just to the Freys but to the people of Westeros under his guidance and protection. By giving in to his own base desires and then betraying the Freys to assuage his own conscience, he shatters alliances and creates enmity that impairs cooperation in preparations for Winter's approach. This increases the likelihood that many of Robb's subjects—or perhaps most of them—will not survive. This sin is perhaps magnified by the fact that Robb is a Stark, and he has been hearing and saying the Stark motto his entire life.

Robb shows some level of recognition of his wrongs and has a plan to make amends to the Freys; however, he does not understand the level or depth of their offense at his betrayal. He makes a simplistic attempt to appease their anger by securing a marriage between one of Frey's daughters and Edmure Tully, but he ends up a guest at the Freys' Red Wedding. Robb and his men are butchered, and Robb's corpse is desecrated with the head of Grey Wind, his direwolf, sewn onto its shoulders. The symbolism of this final insult seems to place Robb on par with animals who cannot control lust even when much more is at stake.

Catelyn Stark has many excellent qualities as a human being, including a loving nature, fierce loyalty, and keen intelligence. She also has difficulty forgiving, demonstrates a tendency to seek vengeance, and acts on impulse. When in an emotional state, Catelyn lashes out, without significant attention to the long-range consequences of her tantrums. She cannot see past her own need for retribution, and never truly acknowledges her own faults, to herself or to anyone else.

Catelyn's list of wrongs begins to mount early in *A Game of Thrones*. She never finds it in her otherwise large heart to show Jon Snow, the bastard child in her care, any form of acceptance and cannot seem to forgive her husband for bringing the boy to live at Winterfell. Through her coldness to Jon, she exacts revenge on him for being in her life and makes an inno-cent child pay for her unhappiness. Her penchant toward both vengeance and rash, emotionally-driven action becomes more obvious when she erroneously arrests and imprisons Tyrion Lannister to avenge the assault on her son Brandon. Her cap-ture of a Lannister endangers her husband, and ultimately her whole family—and the event becomes a catalyst for war. Despite living with and loving some of the Starks for most of her adult life, Catelyn dishonors their purpose as Wardens of the North. She pursues her own emotional satisfaction and commits an ultimate sin in Westeros by further dividing society and greatly damaging the chances that inhabitants can make themselves ready for Winter.

Catelyn's penalties for her impulsive actions and her failure to understand her own faults are steep: the execution of her hus-band and the death (real and supposed) of her children. These losses do not spark understanding of how her rash choices led to disaster, and Catelyn does not embark on a path to redemp-tion. In fact, prior to her death, she commits an emotion-laced atrocity, using Walder Frey's intellectually impaired grandson Jinglebell as a hostage during the Red Wedding, then cutting his throat as Robb Stark dies. With this act, she further tarnishes her character and her soul. When she rises from death after three days in the river, she becomes Lady Stoneheart. This vengeance-obsessed incarnation makes physically manifest the coldness she showed Jon and the ugliness she demonstrated in murder-ing Jinglebell. Lady Stoneheart is hard and devoid of emotion, obsessed only with retribution against her perceived enemies. In death, Catelyn becomes little more than a scarred and merciless reflection of her former self. There is little ambiguity in the fate she suffers, as her body and mind are given wholly over to their darker nature.

If ever a literary character deserved penalty instead of redemption, Joffrey Baratheon would be the boy. Spoiled and indulged by emotionally absent parents, he enjoys bullying and torturing any creature he perceives to be beneath him in status—which encompasses most living things in Westeros. It would be faster to list Joffrey's positives than his negatives, since he has so few of them. In fact, only the Lannister good looks and a dash of superficial charm come to mind. He is narcissistic and devoid of the capacity to love. Not surprisingly, he has no inkling of his own weaknesses, and he does nothing but sow division amongst the people he swears to protect as first their crown prince, and then their king.

Early on in *A Game of Thrones*, Joffrey hires an assassin to complete the murder of Brandon Stark, a deed that is blamed on Tyrion Lannister. This deepens the growing enmity between House Stark and House Lannister. He then assaults Arya Stark and her friend Mycah, resulting in the execution of both Mycah and Sansa's direwolf, Lady. Joffrey's evils only multiply, and in short order, he has Sansa's father beheaded while she watches. Thereafter, he forces her to look at her father's impaled head and has her beaten by his Kingsguard for any perceived disobedience. In *A Storm of Swords*, he tosses Sansa away like rubbish and marries Margaery Tyrell to cement an alliance, all the while making it clear he will bed Sansa any time and with any measure of cruelty he chooses. At the pinnacle of his power, when he believes he is above everyone at his court and the laws of his own land, Joffrey chokes to death, poisoned at his own wedding feast. His biological parents scarcely mourn his passing, choosing instead to copulate in front of his corpse when they are reunited after a separation.

While Joffrey Baratheon is an obvious candidate for such a final humbling by the retributive justice that occurs in Westeros, Robb Stark and Catelyn Stark faced similar ultimate punishments for betraying their honor and acting in ways that further divide an already chaotic and crippled society. Westeros must heal itself and cooperate to survive its long and deadly trial of snow, darkness, and the walking dead. Winter is coming, and these three characters failed to honor this most fundamental and essential reality of their world, closing off the possibility of their own salvation.

The Summer Path

Other characters in A Song of Ice and Fire appear to have more potential for developing insight, and thus redeeming themselves from previous sins. Davos Seaworth is perhaps the most simplistic example of a character with realistic self-appraisal. Born to filth and risen to the rank of smuggler, Davos becomes the most skilled and revered brigand in the Seven Kingdoms. During the great rebellion that precedes A Game of Thrones, he runs blockades with his pirate ship, singlehandedly saving Stannis Baratheon and the knights of Storm's End from death by starvation, earning himself the nickname of the Onion Knight. Stannis honors him for this deed with lands and a title—but also exacts sentence for

Seaworth's past crimes by hacking off the first joint of all the fingers on his left hand.

A true man of his era, Seaworth recognizes his own prior follies and declares this a just punishment. He asks only that Stannis swing the blade himself. Seaworth stands as an example of a man who understands his sins, and is willing to do penance. Though harsh, his sentence leaves him alive and able to pursue his own hero's journey as the books progress. In his current work for Stannis, Seaworth is attempting to bring unity and cooperation, which will be essential to the survival of every soul in the Seven Kingdoms. It will be interesting to see what role he may play in the destruction of Winter's evils when they finally come to threaten all of Westeros.

Sansa Stark—ah, what a complicated and initially deluded young woman! In *A Game of Thrones*, readers find Sansa immature, selfish, and far too easily influenced by fantasies of wealth and ideal love. She has difficulty separating fantasy from reality, and her loyalty to those who love her is never absolute but rather is buffeted by the strength of the personalities around her. Her dreams seem to be coming true when, betrothed to heir-to-the-throne Joffrey Baratheon, she heads off to King's Landing with her father and sister to begin an exciting life as a queen-in-waiting. Of course, it is not long before her pretty fantasies unravel. She sees Joffrey's cruelty in his attack on her sister and her sister's friend, yet she cannot bring herself to do the right thing and speak the truth against him. This failure results in the execution of her direwolf Lady.

Sadly for the Stark family, Sansa learns slowly. Despite clear evidence of Joffrey's sadism and Cersei's perfidy, when Ned

Stark attempts to send Sansa back to Winterfell, she commits the unforgivable sin in Westeros. She focuses on her own personal wishes instead of the well-being of her family or the people she imagines she will one day serve as queen. She flees to Cersei and tells her of Ned's plans, setting in motion her father's arrest and the events that will directly explode into civil war in the Seven Kingdoms. The consequences of this selfish choice are harsh: being forced to witness the beheading of her father—and worse, becoming Joffrey's prisoner and personal whipping girl. She continues her betrayal of House Stark and its words, but now in form only, because she sees that Cersei and Joffrey are evil.

In *A Clash of Kings*, Sansa begins to show maturity during the Battle of the Blackwater, when she comforts other women trapped with her in the Great Sept of Baelor and sows unity, comfort, and strength instead of discord—far more than Queen Cersei can manage. At the conclusion of this battle, Sansa shows more growth still when she puts aside her own selfish perceptions and concerns and instead prays for Sandor Clegane, the Hound, asking, "*Save him if you can, and gentle the rage inside him.*"

Her courage growing, Sansa moves on to an act of outright bravery in *A Storm of Swords*. In a private meeting with the Tyrell matrons, despite extreme risk to herself, she tells the truth about Joffrey's character, naming him a monster. In doing so, she attempts to save Margaery Tyrell from his sadism and, indirectly, the kingdom from the disunity that will foment when Joffrey visits his cruelty on the woman. Joffrey's death by poisoning and Sansa's marriage (albeit forced) to Tyrion Lannister, the one person in the Red Keep who might protect her, seem to be fairly immediate improvements in her situation following this right and selfless action. She then escapes the Lannisters, but unfortunately winds up at the Eyrie under the tutelage of Petyr "Littlefinger" Baelish, and initially at the mercy of her mad aunt, Lysa Tully Arryn. In *A Feast for Crows*, we see little of Sansa, but it is clear she has taken over the duties as female head of household at the Eyrie, and that she is learning much about the type of political intrigue Baelish favors. Her destination on the path to redemption is far from clear, but at least she has the potential to keep walking, if she can keep herself grounded in reality and remember, as others must, that Winter is coming.

Described as having "hair as bright as beaten gold," but "a smile that cut like a knife," Jaime Lannister is known alternately as "The Lion of Lannister" and "Kingslayer." Wealthy, powerful, and narcissistic, Jaime is famous for his skills with the sword and infamous for betraying the most sacred oath he ever swore. He shamelessly commits incest with his twin sister Cersei, and he's happy to pass off his three bastard children as legitimate heirs to the throne of Westeros.

Readers of A Song of Ice and Fire see his basest elements first: arrogance, dishonesty, disregard for social custom and decency, and a remorseless willingness to go to any lengths to protect what he values. After he nearly slays young Brandon Stark to protect the secret of his relationship with Cersei, Jaime goes on later in the story to lead the Lannister guards in an attack on Ned Stark in the streets of King's Landing. He then imprisons Catelyn's brother Edmure and lays siege to Catelyn's beloved home of Riverrun. By this time, most readers have abandoned him as absolutely evil, utterly unlikable, and beyond salvation. In the typically unforgiving cosmology of Westeros, he fosters tremendous disunity, and helps to cripple the Seven Kingdoms as it should be preparing for Winter. Despite these grievous and even unforgivable sins, Jaime Lannister, seemingly like all characters in Westeros, has opportunities for salvation, if he chooses to exploit them and endure the suffering necessary to save his soul.

The roots of Jaime Lannister's suffering actually curl back to the beginnings of his sexual relationship with his twin sister. His incest violates ultimate prohibitions in our world, but in Westeros, it does not carry quite the same stigma due to the historical practices of royal families such as the Targaryens, who routinely married sister to brother to preserve what they believed to be their magical blood. The Lannisters, dysfunctional at best, continue this narcissistic tradition, viewing themselves as far above all other citizens of Westeros. Though shocking to some reader sensibilities, incest itself likely does not constitute grievous sin in the cosmology of Westeros; however, the discord fostered by Jaime's dishonesty and violence in the protection of his incestuous relationship constitute serious transgressions.

Jaime's love for Cersei appears to be genuine; he is never unfaithful to her. Still, it begins to lead him to pain when he accepts her advice and becomes the youngest member of the Kingsguard, at least in part to remain close to her and free from obligations to other women. Jaime feels deeply honored by the appointment, but he quickly realizes that the honor is hollow because his appointment is merely a ploy of Aerys Targaryen to strike at Jaime's father and rob the elder Lannister of his favored heir. Lannister reacts to the appointment by returning to Casterly Rock, taking Cersei with him. Jaime retains his glorious public position in the eyes of the smallfolk in Westeros. Privately, he is alone and without his love, and filled with the realization that he is being used as a pawn. This loss and humiliation serve as the first of many wounds to his once-robust pride. His outward golden shine masks the tarnish beneath, and his sarcasm makes for thin cover of his mounting self-hatred.

Jaime's doubt and confusion only grow when the king's madness and cruelty manifest across every day of Jaime's life, a trauma so severe that he learns to dissociate—a skill he later teaches his son Tommen, telling him, "The world is full of horrors, Tommen. You can fight them, or laugh at them, or [...] go away inside" (*A Feast for Crows*). Here again, while Jaime maintains outward power, he seems to understand the extent of his own powerlessness and to force himself to accept the bitter role of court pawn and white-robed fool.

Just before the opening of *A Game of Thrones*, Jaime must choose between keeping his sacred vow to protect a depraved and insane ruler and allowing the slaughter of his father, his father's men, and most of the residents of King's Landing. He elects to kill the king under his protection. By the underlying moral principle in Westeros—that unity and the good of society must come first for the survival of everyone in the kingdom—this murder is righteous. Jaime seems to sense this, even if his own moral failings leave him unable to understand it. Afterward, he takes a seat on the Iron Throne—but he makes no move to claim it. He hands it over to Ned Stark and Robert Baratheon without a battle, creating unity and seeing to the good of the whole, even if he probably does not grasp the importance of his choice.

At the close of *A Game of Thrones*, Jaime Lannister's rout of Riverrun takes a bad turn and he finds himself a prisoner of the vengeful Catelyn Stark. Fate deals Jaime another blow to his ego when he becomes Lord Commander of the Kingsguard due to the dismissal of his predecessor—but he is still a prisoner of Riverrun and cannot assume the role he dreamed of taking for most of his childhood. This situation makes the appointment a cruel joke, undermining Jaime's self-respect by underscoring both his helplessness and his uselessness.

Thus, by the opening of *A Clash of Kings*, Jaime has lost his freedom, the bulk of his political power, and the remaining shreds of his pride and self-respect. During the course of this novel, he loses his famed good looks, as well. When he emerges from Riverrun's dungeons, he is a gaunt shadow of himself, and he must shave his golden hair to avoid recognition on the journey he undertakes to save Sansa Stark. He also loses Cersei, who takes other lovers without thought to wounding Jaime's feelings. These are high costs for a man like Jaime Lannister, but he has more to pay. Enter Brienne of Tarth, a female knight who becomes Jaime's personal torturer by showing him at every possible turn how an honorable and honest warrior should behave. Brienne is Jaime's "morality pet," a living embodiment of the noble knight Jaime should have been and which he might become if he chooses an honorable path henceforth.

Jaime again loses his freedom when he and Brienne are taken prisoner by Vargo Hoat and his Brave Companions. Like the Mad King, Hoat uses Jaime as a pawn and cuts off Jaime's sword hand in hopes that his superior, Roose Bolton, will be blamed. Jaime is forced to wear his rotting hand around his neck. All that Jaime Lannister once was—handsome, powerful, strong, skilled with the blade—has now been destroyed. He enters a dark landscape of hopelessness and self-loathing.

Rescue eventually comes for Jaime, but no sooner is he free than he begins to realize fundamental aspects of his character and priorities have changed. He chooses to place himself at risk and return to potential captivity in order to rescue Brienne from dishonor and death. He saves her life again when they arrive at King's Landing, and gives her the sword Oathkeeper with the charge of protecting Sansa Stark, as he had sworn to do. Though he briefly tries to rekindle his relationship with Cersei, he quickly sees that she does not love him as he has loved her, and that she remains selfish and treacherous. Jaime then does the previously unthinkable—he stands up to his father and refuses to separate himself from the Kingsguard. Instead, in a repudiation of pride and a rejection of selfishness, he dons the white again, this time in earnest.

By the end of *A Storm of Swords*, it is clear that Jaime's actions are no longer focused on himself and his personal gain. This transition completes itself in *A Feast for Crows*, when he finds the strength to leave his scheming sister Cersei to her fate after she runs afoul of a sect of religious zealots. He spends most of this tale and *A Dance with Dragons* bringing battles to an end around Westeros, creating unity—the ultimate act of good in a society about to face dangers that only cooperation can defeat. We see him accept the humbling of the loss of his sword hand and begin to work to reform himself as a competent, though no longer brilliant, fighter. He is no longer the Kingslayer *or* the Lion of Lannister. He is Jaime and, as yet, nothing more.

Davos Seaworth, Sansa Stark, and Jaime Lannister appear to be on a similar trajectory. Whether their journeys will lead them to eventual salvation or utter destruction because of flaws and sins they cannot or will not overcome remains to be seen; however, it is clear that in Westeros, characters can find their way to good if they are willing to pay the brutal price.

Unchanging Seasons

Unlike the almost allegorical worlds of J.R.R. Tolkien and his contemporaries, which are imbued with unambiguous representations of good and evil, Westeros defines these concepts with more subtlety and realism, grounded in the fact that Winter is coming, and with it a host of horrors, making the very survival of society dependent upon inhabitants cooperating and acting for the benefit of the whole instead of pursuing more selfish or individualistic aims. As such, what is "good" in Westeros supports unity, and what is "bad" sows discord and disrupts chances for survival. Honesty, humility, honor, and other characteristics that allow people to work closely together without divisive conflict have value in this society.

Sorting through the issues of morality in A Song of Ice and Fire is not simplistic, especially since readers view the Seven Kingdoms through the flawed perceptions of its inhabitants, most of whom are too young to remember an actual Winter, and further filter these perceptions through our own biases. This does not mean that the world is amoral, or that characters do not engage in fundamental struggles to make right and moral choices. Through the destruction of some characters and the redemption of others, we see a cosmology at work in Martin's world that is anything but relativistic or nihilistic.

◆ ◆ ◆

SUSAN VAUGHT lives with her family and her many pets (including a very bossy parrot) on a small poultry farm in western Kentucky. She works as Director of Psychological Services at a state psychiatric hospital and spends her evenings and weekends furiously scribbling and typing life into novels, short stories, and poems. She has written a number of fantasies for young adults, including the award-winning and historical *Stormwitch* and the epic Oathbreaker books: *Assassin's Apprentice* and *A Prince Among Killers*, co-authored with her son JB Redmond. She has also written *Trigger*, *Big Fat Manifesto*, *Exposed*, and *Going Underground*, all contemporary novels drawing from her experiences and her work as a neuropsychologist. Her upcoming contemporary release from Bloomsbury USA, *Freaks Like Us*, will hit the shelves in September 2012.

◆ ANDREW ZIMMERMAN JONES ◆

OF DIREWOLVES AND GODS

EVIDENCE FROM NEUROLOGY SUGGESTS that our brains are wired to believe things even without any evidence. The dominant explanation is that it's a better survival mechanism to believe a sound or a flicker of motion has meaning than to ignore it. In a world where a hungry lion (and not the Lannister type) might be lying in wait behind any given bush, this hardwired tendency to assume significance offers a slight advantage in seeing the next sunrise.

Unfortunately, this same wiring kicks in even when there isn't a lion, a Lannister, or even a sound to trigger it. Our brains naturally assume that perceived patterns have meaning, even if there's no proof that they do. This inherent search for meaning is the psychological and neurological basis for much human superstition.

I've always been pleased to find that meaning made manifest within fantasy literature. Through fantasy, I escape to worlds that conform to these intuitions about how things should be. These imaginary worlds often contain greater meaning, expressed by strong, tangible forces of good and evil. Wishes can come true. Magic works. Gods even manifest their wonders in the world for all to see. The first chapters of *A Game of Thrones* promise an escape to just such a realm.

It turns out, though, that the people of the Seven Kingdoms really don't inhabit this sort of fantasy world at all. Much like us, they have no regular or direct interactive access to their deities. Theirs is a world of neither the mythical philandering, lightning-hurling Zeus nor the power-granting deities of any staple *Dungeons & Dragons* setting. Magic exists in Westeros, but it is rare and mostly ephemeral, a distant memory of the past. With a handful of flamboyant exceptions, the gods don't imbue their priests and followers with supernatural powers. Westeros is filled with religions and exotic gods, but believers have to take a lot on faith—a faith that is often unrewarding. The good and the bad may worship the same set of gods. Regardless of the deities worshipped, the certainty is this: tragedy will ultimately befall you, and the gods rarely hold it at bay, even for the noblest of souls.

In fact, the religions portrayed in A Song of Ice and Fire are reflections of the religions in our own world. They require a leap of faith, because the effects of belief are so intangible. The religions of Westeros claim to dictate absolute, perfect truths through imprecise, flawed institutions and beings—just like the religions we encounter every day.

A Direwolf Omen

The capricious nature of the putative Westerosi gods can be seen very early in the series, in the scene that likely hooked most readers. Or, at least, the scene that hooked me.

The prologue of *A Game of Thrones* was okay. Rangers out scouting frozen northern lands are accosted by curious creatures, presumably undead in some fashion. Spooky stuff. Interesting enough to keep you reading, for sure, but hardly gripping enough to make it different from any of hundreds of other fantasy series.

Then came the direwolves.

In the first chapter where we meet the Stark family, a direwolf is found dead, sparking the soon-to-be-ill-fated Jory to proclaim, "It is a sign." Jon Snow is more explicit, though, when he says to his father, "You have five trueborn children [. . .]. Three sons, two daughters. The direwolf is the sigil of your House. Your children were meant to have these pups, my lord."

The hint of destiny lingers over the scene. Powerful forces seem to link the young Stark children together with these direwolves. At this point in the book, with so little knowledge of the setting, the fantasy reader is inclined to believe that this connection has otherworldly significance and that belief is made all the stronger when Jon then discovers an albino pup, declaring, "This one belongs to me." The direwolves not only match Ned Stark's trueborn children, but there is also an outsider for the bastard son. Our minds are wired to look for meanings in patterns, and this pattern just begs to be more than mere coincidence.

Catelyn sees something much more dire in this event than the arrival of pets: "[A] direwolf dead in the snow, a broken antler in its throat. Dread coiled within her like a snake, but she forced herself to smile at this man she loved, this man who put no faith in signs." This does prove to be ominous, a sign of grim things to come, as attested by the ultimate fate of Ned Stark at the command of Joffrey (a broken antler if ever there were one).

But what of the direwolf pups themselves? As a reader, I placed a lot of weight on the greater significance of the direwolves and on Jon's proclamation that the "children were meant to have these pups." I anticipated the direwolves playing a crucial role in the events yet to unfold. After all, surely such a curious origin meant they were intended for great things.

In that respect, I've found the direwolves to be a great disappointment.

Bran's direwolf, Summer, proves his worth early on, when he rescues Lady Catelyn and protects Bran from an assassination attempt. Certainly Ghost is a useful companion to Jon Snow as he takes the black. And Robb Stark's rise as King in the North is predicated, in no small part, on his legendary status as "the young wolf," fighting alongside Grey Wind.

Even by the conclusion of the first book, though, the direwolves have become, at best, background elements of the Stark children, rather than significant components of the story itself. Two are lost—one killed and one chased off—even before the Starks reach King's Landing. And now, five books into the series, the promise of the direwolves seems even more distant. Grey Wind's fate matched that of Robb, the two murdered under a flag of truce then grafted together in a twisted mockery of their living connection. Arya has been separated from Nymeria for years, yet maintains hints of a vague psychic link. The connections of Bran and Jon to their wolves is substantially different, and stronger, but have yet to really impact the larger storyline. Ghost vanishes for nearly half of *A Storm of Swords* and Jon seems barely fazed by it, even as he's coming to terms with being a warg. Aside from Bran's, the wolves are largely expendable.

And that, ultimately, is the curious thing about the direwolves. They are presented as this promise, a representation of some sort of divine prophecy and intervention. The discovery scene early in *A Game of Thrones* seems to suggest that the wolves are intended for the children, presumably as protection. When Summer defends Bran and Catelyn, divine powers seem to be intervening to protect the young Stark family, but the protection has been inconsistent in the story since.

The gods of Westeros are as disappointing as the direwolves. Whether present, absent, or outright dead, the deities never quite live up to the expectations of those who believe in them. In fact, it's really a wonder that they have any followers at all.

The Gods of Westeros

The situation is muddled because Westeros is home to so very many gods. Let's take a quick inventory:

> **Old Gods:** The northmen worship ancient gods of stone and earth and tree, as were worshipped by the children of the forest in ancient days. There appears to be no formal priesthood for these gods, and their places of worship are at special weirwood trees with faces carved in

them. The First Men continued this tradition by planting a single weirwood, called a heart tree, in godswoods at their noble houses throughout Westeros.

The Seven: With the Andal invasion, which occured over six thousand years before the events in the novels, came the religion of the Faith of the Seven. The seven deities are reflections of each other, similar to the concept of the Trinity in mainstream modern Christianity, though they also contain analogs to elements of paganism. They are: Father, Mother, Warrior, Maiden, Smith, Crone, and Stranger.

The Drowned God: The Ironborn of the Iron Islands worship a brutal deity called the Drowned God. Belief in the Drowned God informs all of their traditions, especially their pirate culture, because it leads them to treat conquest, rape, and plunder as a divine act.

R'hllor, Lord of Light: R'hllor is a foreign god that is becoming more dominant in Westeros, mostly through the militant conversion imposed by Stannis Baratheon. Of all the gods, R'hllor is the one in whose name the most overt supernatural wonders have been invoked.

The Many-Faced God: Though not based in Westeros, this is an amalgamated religion that sees the death gods of all faiths as representing a single being. The followers of the Many-Faced God form a cult, the Faceless Men, which teaches assassination as a religious practice. The cultists appear to be granted the power to alter their appearance. The Stranger of the Seven is considered one of the faces of the Many-Faced God.

The Great Other: Priests of R'hllor indicate that there is another dark god "whose name must not be spoken." This god is the antithesis of R'hllor, representing darkness, cold, and death.

There are other gods mentioned throughout the series, mostly in reference to those worshipped within the Free Cities and Valyria, but they have less of a bearing on the book's central events than these.

Not all epic fantasies go to so great a length to incorporate clear and diverse religious structures into their worlds. Read through Tolkien, for example, and you will find hardly a mention of a priesthood or specific religious doctrine, despite the strong evidence of religious themes and overt manifestations of forces both good and evil. The closest thing to a deity we run across in Middle-earth is Tom Bombadil and, frankly, he seems like he'd be indifferent to any form of worship directed his way.

Even in series that contain specific religious traditions and orders—such as Robert Jordan's Wheel of Time books—these traditions often align in clearer ways with the positive and negative forces at the heart of the universe. Those forces may be defined as good and evil, law and chaos, or some other spectrum, but religions often have relatively clear places within the ethical cosmology.

The lines between good and evil are not nearly so clear within Westeros. Or rather, there is a very clear line, but it's a physical one, not a religious one. The Wall stands between the dark, cold Others and the realm of man. Despite the presence of the Free Folk north of the Wall, the cosmology of Westeros seems to define this domain as belonging to the world's evil forces. It is far less clear that an equivalent force of good is at work south of the Wall.

The metaphysical threat in the series, from the very first page, has been the Others north of the Wall, but this threat remains largely absent from most of the major plotlines developing in the series. The readers and Jon Snow know of the danger, but the threat's escalation has been glacial in its progression compared to the whirlwind of activity in King's Landing or even Valyria. Most characters don't even really believe that the Others exist, and those who do favor conflicting interpretations of what they are.

There is no ambiguity about their nature among the R'hllor priests. To them, the Others serve R'hllor's nemesis, the Great Other, reminiscent of the Christian split between God and Satan. The priest Moqorro explicitly says to the Ironborn, "Your Drowned God is a demon. [. . .] He is no more than a thrall of the Other, the dark god whose name must not be spoken" (*A Dance with Dragons*). To the Lord of Light's followers, all faiths but R'hllor represent the Great Other.

The other faiths seem to at least leave open some form of broader polytheism. This is explicit in the case of the Faceless Men and the Faith of the Seven, but for other religions it is a bit less clear. For example, worshippers of the Drowned God may not necessarily think the Seven don't exist; they just think that their god is superior.

Though some Westerosi religions are more sympathetic than others, we're given hints that they all may contain elements of truth. Characters believe or disbelieve in the gods based on their own temperaments, not because they typically have any real reason to think that one has more validity than the others.

Hearing the Voice of Gods

One of the chief teachings of most religions is that the deity or dieties communicate their will to devotees in some meaningful way. Prophecy, even if only in the form of strong intuitions and inner spiritual guidance, seems almost a requirement of religion. Merely from a practical standpoint, a religion that claimed its deities remained absolutely silent to the faithful would have a serious recruiting disadvantage.

The will of the gods is difficult to interpret in Westeros. Beyond the direwolves omen, the track record of accurate prophecies has been much spottier. Perhaps Ned Stark is wrong to "put no faith in signs," but the series as a whole implies that prophecies are not statistically safe bets. This isn't a slip of the author, because the story specifically addresses the prophetic fumbles.

A Clash of Kings begins with an ominous red asteroid hurtling through the sky, but various individuals interpret the sign as a portent of very different things. None of the interpretations really seem to be borne out by subsequent events.

One has to imagine that Melisandre is surprised at the mismatch between the victories she's seen in her flames and those she's witnessed in real life. When she does finally let her air of confidence slip, she justifies the failure of the world to match her prophecies by placing the blame not upon her perfect and infallible Lord of Light, but upon herself. "The vision was a true one. It was my reading that was false. I am as mortal as you, Jon Snow. All mortals err" (*A Dance with Dragons*).

There are more cynical views of prophecy, pointing the finger of blame at the prophecy rather than the prophet. Tyrion

Lannister says, "Prophecy is like a half-trained mule. [. . .] It looks as though it might be useful, but the moment you trust in it, it kicks you in the head" (*A Dance with Dragons*). But it is Archmaester Marwyn who really gets the prize for impuning prophecy with a graphic and colorful analogy:

> "Gorghan of Old Ghis once wrote that a prophecy is like a treacherous woman. She takes your member in her mouth, and you moan with the pleasure of it and think, how sweet, how fine, how good this is . . . and then her teeth snap shut and your moans turn to screams. That is the nature of prophecy, said Gorghan. Prophecy will bite your prick off every time." (*A Feast for Crows*)

It is significant to note that even the cynical observations do not reject the premise that prophecy can provide a true glimpse of what is to come; instead, they cast doubt on our own ability to wield prophecy in a useful way, even if it is true. Again, the dead direwolf proves illustrative: Catelyn urges Ned to accept the position as the King's Hand in large part due to the omen, because she fears that rejecting it will harm Robert's pride. Pricks aren't the only body parts lost by prophecy.

Choosing Your Religion

Much as in our own world, choice of religion in Westeros seems to be a matter more of familial or even regional tradition than personal choice. The faiths of Catelyn and Ned Stark demonstrate a situation in which each remains true to the gods of their ancestors. Despite the fact that they have a septa in charge of the education and care of their daughters, the boys are expected to hold to the faith of their father. This isn't just a Stark tradition, either. Samwell seems to describe a fairly common chain of belief when he identifies the religious lineage of House Tarly: "I was named in the light of the Seven at the sept on Horn Hill, as my father was, and his father, and all the Tarlys for a thousand years" (*A Game of Thrones*).

Still, freedom of religious choice does exist within Westeros, because Samwell then chooses to make his oath to the Night's Watch in the weirwood, beside his new brother, Jon Snow. As Samwell says, "The Seven have never answered my prayers. Perhaps the old gods will" (*A Game of Thrones*).

A Song of Ice and Fire begins presenting a pluralistic, religiously tolerant Westeros, but that tolerance definitely wanes as the series progresses. Stannis Baratheon becomes a radical devotee of R'hllor, forcing religious conversion as part of fealty oaths and conquests, and Cersei reinstates the militant orders of the Faith of the Seven, the Warrior's Sons and the Poor Fellows, which ultimately gain enough power to depose her on their own authority. This trend toward theocratic militarism within Westeros had been weeded out in centuries past and its return does not bode well for the world.

Assuming that one avoids coercion, it's unclear that a new arrival in Westeros would find any compelling reason to follow any religion, except for social advantages. Catelyn Stark, a devout follower of the Seven, "had more faith in a maester's learning than a septon's prayers" (*A Game of Thrones*) when it comes to medical care. Even Asha—as Ironborn as they come—laments,

"The Drowned God did not answer. He seldom did. That was the trouble with gods" (*A Dance with Dragons*). Throughout Westeros, it seems that the gods may be worshipped, but they can hardly be relied upon to deliver aid when it is most needed.

The one exception may be R'hllor, who works the most overt miracles in his name. However, the nature of R'hllor's miracles bring into question whether he's truly the noble Lord of Light that his followers proclaim. Who really wants to worship a god that gives birth to murderous shadow-creatures? If you were trying to put faith in a moral deity, R'hllor might not be your top pick.

The strongest voice in favor of R'hllor's role as supreme and exclusively good deity is Melisandre, but her credibility is dubious, in no small part because she is introduced by murdering an elderly maester. That act is arguably self-defense, though her gleeful demeanor still lingers unfavorably. Beyond that, we know that she's unapologetically murdered at least three men and advocated the ritual sacrifice of children.

When Ser Davos says, "It seems to me that most men are grey," Melisandre replies: "If half an onion is black with rot, it is a rotten onion. A man is good, or he is evil" (*A Clash of Kings*). This philosophy doesn't bode well for either Melisandre or R'hllor, both of whom certainly seem to have some rot about them.

In fact, the entire series forces Melisandre's moral absolutism into doubt, as we are regularly given characters who seem to be thoroughly vile but are later revealed to have noble aspects to their nature—and vice versa. Part of the draw of the books is that the characters are complex and multifaceted, with flaws and virtues constantly in conflict. Even the heartless Cersei Lannister is portrayed as a once-frightened child who lost out on the chance at a great destiny and also as a fiercely protective mother, both traits that engender some measure of empathy—just enough to keep the reader from cheering unconditionally at her degrading downfall.

In a world where every person is, in fact, grey, where good and evil are found cohabiting in every noble, knight, and peasant, why would it be any different among the gods? Really, it only makes sense that it would be hard to tell the good from the bad. And what option does that leave to the person looking for a god to worship?

Rejecting the Gods

One path left open is that taken by Tyrion. "If I could pray with my cock, I'd be much more religious" (*A Clash of Kings*), he notes, but short of that, he has no particular use for gods. His brother Jaime has pretty much gone the same route. If ever there was a time when Jaime embraced the worship of the gods, it has long since passed. When his hostage, Hoster Blackwood, declares rather uncertainly, "The gods are good," Jaime's immediate thought is "*You go on believing that*" (*A Dance with Dragons*).

Strictly speaking, these characters haven't rejected the existence of gods. They aren't necessarily atheists, but they reside somewhere on the agnostic spectrum. The religious people they run across seem peculiar to them, unfathomable in their desire to embrace deities that, if they exist, seem at best capricious and at worst outright malicious.

Of the Lannister siblings, Cersei, curiously enough, has the most faith in the divine powers. She believes that she was prophesied by the gods to become queen of the Seven Kingdoms, yet this doesn't stop her from committing incest in a sept (in front of her son's corpse, no less) or murdering the High Septon. And those are just her offenses specifically against the Faith of the Seven.

Even those characters who have clung more strongly to their religious convictions don't seem to receive any particular reward for it. The most extreme examples of divine favor—the resurrections of Beric Dondarrion and ultimately Catelyn Stark—aren't the sort of rewards that most of us would pray for.

The ambiguous status of religion in the series seems an intentional act on the part of George R.R. Martin, who described himself in a July 2011 *Entertainment Weekly* interview as a "lapsed Catholic" and acknowledged that most would call him "an atheist or agnostic." He went on to say, "And as for the gods, I've never been satisfied by any of the answers that are given. If there really is a benevolent loving god, why is the world full of rape and torture? Why do we even have pain? I was taught pain is to let us know when our body is breaking down. Well, why couldn't we have a light? Like a dashboard light? If Chevrolet could come up with that, why couldn't God? Why is agony a good way to handle things?"

Perception, Power, and Religion

Despite the fact that they rarely live up to expectations, the gods of Westeros wield immense power, even if they themselves cannot typically be bothered to show up and help move things along. In crafting his own gods, Martin has avoided the easy way out. He could have provided satisfying answers, by building a world in which gods of good grant healing and gods of evil grant dominion over legions of undead. That isn't Westeros, though. The religions he crafts are not obviously true and accessible but are instead just as obscure and subjective as those we practice. Much like the direwolves, maybe it's enough to know that the gods just *might* be lurking in the wings, ready to spring into action at a moment's notice.

Ultimately, religious faith isn't really about the end result; it's about the *perception* of the end result. Despite the lack of evidence, we are driven to see meaning in the patterns of the world around us. Religion's power comes, at least in part, from offering us the meaning we are hardwired to seek. Whatever else it may be, religion provides a ready-made narrative around which we can build our lives. It places our individual and group suffering and accomplishments in a more significant context. These beliefs are the ultimate source of religious power and authority in this world.

Or, as summed up more succinctly by Varys in *A Clash of Kings*: "Power resides where men *believe* it resides. No more and no less."

◆ ◆ ◆

ANDREW ZIMMERMAN JONES is an author and editor of both fiction and nonfiction. He studied physics, philosophy, and mathematics (along with a couple of religion courses) at Wabash College and has earned a Master's degree in Mathematics Education from Purdue University. Andrew has been a finalist in the L. Ron Hubbard's Writers of the Future Contest, received Honorable Mention in the 2011 Writer's Digest Science Fiction/Fantasy Competition, and previously appeared in Smart Pop Books' anthology *Inside Joss' Dollhouse*. He's the author of *String Theory for Dummies*, the About.com Physics Guide, and a contributing editor to *Black Gate* fantasy adventure magazine. Andrew is a member of the National Association of Science Writers, American Mensa, and Toastmasters International. He lives in central Indiana with his wife, two young sons, two cats, and five chickens. Links to his work and various online personas can be reached through his website at azjones.info.

◆ JESSE SCOBLE ◆

A SWORD WITHOUT A HILT

The Dangers of Magic in (and to) Westeros

GEORGE R.R. MARTIN'S A Song of Ice and Fire has been a success, in large part, because it has recaptured fans of the fantasy
genre who had grown bored and moved away from the standard
fare, and because it has reached a wide audience of those who
traditionally do not read or watch fantasy genre entertainment.
In an interview with the MTV Movies Blog, HBO Showrunner
David Benioff said, "I think some people think, 'Oh, I don't want
to watch a fantasy show because I'm not that into magic,' but one
of the things that is great about George's books is that they don't
rely overly much on magic." Similarly, Tor blogger Leigh Butler
expressed the sentiment that Martin seemed almost afraid to
commit, in terms of how much magic to put in the series. In
her penultimate "A Read of Ice and Fire" post, Leigh's reaction

to the birth of the dragons was: "Daaaamn, y'all. So apparently magic is not so much nonexistent in Martin's world after all!"

What's intriguing about this is that Martin's world of the Seven Kingdoms is steeped in magic. But it is not used in a "traditional fantasy" sense.

By "traditional fantasy," I'm speaking of the body of tales and entertainments that traces its roots back to Robert E. Howard's Conan stories, J.R.R. Tolkien's The Lord of the Rings, and C.S. Lewis's Chronicles of Narnia, and which has come to encompass things like *Dungeons & Dragons* and the predictable, often-clichéd yarns of elves, dwarfs, orcs, and goblins. In the 1962 essay "Conan's Imitators," L. Sprague de Camp called these sorts of works "sword & sorcery," which he defined as "stories laid in an imaginary pre-industrial setting wherein, although the supernatural played an important part, the accent was on action, adventure, and heroism."

Many readers, myself included, grew up on a diet of this kind of fantasy, graduated into roleplaying games, but then put away such "childish things" as the demands of life and the workaday world took over. One of the reasons that many fans grow out of the fantasy genre is because the bookshelves have been overpopulated with unimaginative worlds recycling the same old ideas. If every adventurer has a backpack full of enchanted swords; a magic ring on every finger; and spells to hurl fireballs and magic missiles, as well as to boil coffee, and heal pimples, and maybe even raise the dead, the world becomes boring and dull because of the ubiquitous and predictable nature of the magic.

That's not the case in A Song of Ice and Fire. Though at times the series feels like historical fiction—many readers have drawn apt comparisons to the War of the Roses and the Hundred Years' War—it's the very absence of overt magic that makes the glimpses we see so effective. As Martin wrote in his essay "On Fantasy" (1996), "Reality is the strip malls of Burbank, the smokestacks of Cleveland, a parking garage in Newark. Fantasy is the towers of Minas Tirith, the ancient stones of Gormenghast, the halls of Camelot." Those hints of magic are key to making A Song of Ice and Fire what it is: exotic, mysterious, and dangerous.

Cold Open

A Game of Thrones opens with a scene of magic. Several members of the Night's Watch—Gared, Will, and Ser Waymar Royce—come face-to-face with the dread Others. As the reader wonders if these foes are fantastically garbed humans, some kind of recognizable "alien" like an elf or dark faerie, or something more unusual, Ser Waymar is mercilessly killed. The dead man then stands back up, eyes burning unnaturally blue, and wraps his hands around Will's throat. By opening the series with this scene, Martin announces from the outset that magic does exist in this world and will play a major part in this epic.

After that terrifying introduction of the Others, however, Martin does something unexpected and leaves magic off the stage for many chapters. Instead, he embroils the reader in the stories of the Starks, King Robert, the Lannisters, and a host of bannermen, lesser lords, courtly ladies, and their retinues. Martin further expands the world by introducing the reader and Daenerys Targaryen simultaneously to the Dothraki horselords across the narrow sea. Yet while explicit magic is kept off the page, we see hints and references to the greater role it once played in the world. Magic, we understand, may have only gone underground. And it may well return.

Stories and Superstitions

Westeros is a world where magic has faded from the day-to-day world of nobles and smallfolk alike. The last dragon died out approximately a century and a half before the beginning of *A Game of Thrones*, and magic, it appears, died with it. But the world is still ripe with ritual, superstitious beliefs, artifacts, and stories that have roots in that earlier, more magical time.

In one of the key scenes, early in *A Games of Thrones*, Eddard Stark's party comes upon a dead direwolf bitch, killed by a stag's tine in her throat, and five orphaned puppies in the snow. The direwolf is the symbol of House Stark, and the noble families in Westeros put a great deal of faith in their house symbols and mottos. Jon Snow stays Theon from slaying the pups by suggesting to Lord Eddard that the animals are destined for each of the five trueborn Stark children. When Jon is asked about one for himself, he explains that as a bastard he is not due the same consideration as those of pure blood, but when the sixth pup, an albino outcast, is found, it is just as clear that this direwolf was "meant" for Snow. The characters understand the pups as an omen—one that only seems to be confirmed, to the characters and to us as readers, when House Baratheon, whose symbol is the royal stag, brings about Ned Stark's downfall later in the book. Whether the death of the direwolf and the discovery of her pups is a "true" omen or not, the characters' willingness to put stock in the idea is telling.

Early in *A Game of Thrones*, we also see the architectural wonder of the Wall, a great monument of ice and stone approximately three hundred miles long and seven hundred feet high. Stories say Bran the Builder engineered the Wall, eight thousand years past, weaving spells of protection into it to shield Westeros from the Others and monstrosities from the Lands of Always Winter. Stories tell that magic is the only way to bring down the Wall, as well. The Horn of Winter, or the Horn of Joramun, is an artifact that the wildlings say can not only bring down the Wall, but awaken the giants.

Throughout the opening of the series we see Valyrian steel blades, hear of tantalizing dreams that may be prophetic, and learn the history of a kingdom carved out by dragon fire. Samwell Tarly says warlocks from Qarth bathed him in auroch's blood to make him brave; but he retched, and it did not take. Old Nan tells bedtime stories of the Long Night, the devastating winter where the inhuman Others swept the realm with terror, and Dany hears tales of magic in the far east—Moonsingers of the Jogos Nhai, mages from Asshai, and Dothraki spells of grass and corn and horse. In a way, these early pages are full of magic, but only as myths, legends, and rumors.

Given the aura of unreliability surrounding the subject, it should not be a surprise, then, to learn that the maesters, who are some of the most educated and learned characters in Westeros, have a conflicted relationship with magic. They acknowledge it existed at one time, but few look upon it favorably. Not many study magic enough to gain a Valyrian steel link in their chain, and those who do are often regarded as strange. Still others, like House Stark's Maester Luwin, seem almost jaded and bitter to find no substance in magic.

There is some indication that the maesters, or a conspiratorial subset of them, may have worked to suppress magic in the world. It is unclear how the last dragons died, and while the first legends we learn say Aegon III poisoned them, Archmaester Marwyn tells Sam Tarly a different tale: "'Who do you think killed all the dragons the last time around? Gallant dragonslayers with swords?' He spat. 'The world the Citadel is building has no place in it for sorcery or prophecy or glass candles, much less for dragons'" (*A Feast for Crows*). It's not hard to guess that most maesters would prefer a knowable world of science and logic to a capricious one of magic and glamor. And, of course, magic would certainly be a challenge to the maesters' established positions of power.

All acolytes of the Citadel must stand a final night's vigil in a pitch-black vault before donning their maester's chains. They are permitted no torch or lamp but only a candle of obsidian; they must spend the night in darkness unless they find some way to light the candle. Armen explains, "Even after he has said his vow and donned his chain and gone forth to serve, a maester will think back on the darkness of his vigil and remember how nothing that he did could make the candle burn . . . for even with knowledge, some things are not possible" (*A Feast for Crows*).

But this is not the lesson all take from the vigil. While most of the candles remain unlit, the acolytes holding them left brooding in the dark, there are others, like the one Leo Tyrell describes seeing in Marwyn's chambers in the Citadel, that burns with an unearthly flame. Slowly, despite the weight of history and the maesters' hope that magic is dead, the fantastic intrudes upon the mundane in ways that even the most logic-bound cannot deny.

In still other parts of the world, magic holds an even greater sway.

Beyond the Wall

Stories of magic and potent superstition are especially prevalent, and far more accepted, in the desolate lands north of the Wall. This is where we first see tangible magic in the story, both in the book's opening pages and later, once Jon Snow takes the black. When two brothers of the Night's Watch, Jafer Flowers and Othor, return as undead wights to kill their sworn brothers, it takes Snow and his direwolf, Ghost, to save Lord Commander Mormont—an important scene because it is another early hint that magic is bubbling up at the edges of the world. Jon has seen the Wall and may understand logically that such an architectural marvel could only have been built with magic, but that's ancient history. Facing down a dead man that struggles long after his arm has been severed makes magic, and the supernatural, real.

Wildlings in the north speak freely of giants, wargs, greenseers, and the old gods. Wargs—or skinchangers—are more understood here, as we see in the wildlings Orell and Varamyr Sixskins. So, too, is knowledge of the Others. Mance Rayder, the King-Beyond-the-Wall, seeks a safe haven for his people from their predations, while the Night's Watch suspects the wildling

Craster of sacrificing his male offspring to the cold to keep the Others at bay.

The reasons for the power of magic north of the Wall remain unclear, at least in the story so far. Perhaps the Wall does not quench magic in the far north, or more is retained in the weirwoods of the children of the forest; another theory is that the dark magic of the Others is not as dependent on dragons as the magic practiced south of the Wall. Whatever the cause, though, there's no denying that magic holds a greater sway over the lands beyond the Wall.

Essos and the East

Stories of magic are also much more prominent in the exotic east, in Essos, than they are in Westeros. But it takes one who is part of both lands, yet also not fully of either, to unlock magic across the world. Beautiful Daenerys Targaryen, of the ancient and powerful lineage of Valyria, clings to the stories of her family's grandeur and their magic-rich history. Her ancestral homeland, long since destroyed, is closer geographically and culturally to Essos than to Westeros, and it is said that the Targaryens have features that reflect their links to the magical, what they refer to as "blood of the dragon." Dany never flinches from heat, and she dreams of dragons taking wing and breathing fire. When her patron, Illyrio Mopatis, gives her three petrified dragon eggs as a wedding gift, we can be certain something will hatch from them, either figuratively or literally. As the playwright Anton Chekhov wrote, "One must not put a loaded rifle on the stage if no one is thinking of firing it." So, too, must Martin utilize the dragon eggs. To leave them unexplored, unfired, would be to play a cruel trick upon the reader.

In the buildup to that revelation, Martin introduces us, and Dany, to Mirri Maz Duur, a Lhazareen victim of the rape and pillage of her village, who only survives due to Daenerys's direct intervention. Mirri describes herself as a godswife to the Great Shepherd, and says she learned magic in Asshai-by-the-Shadow to the far east, and healing arts from a maester of the west. The Dothraki have another word for her: *maegi*, a woman who, according to their tales, "lay with demons and practiced the blackest of sorceries, a vile thing, evil and soulless, who came to men in the dark of night and sucked life and strength from their bodies" (*A Game of Thrones*).

Dany turns to Mirri Maz Duur in desperation when Khal Drogo falls to fever and a festering wound. She believes Mirri can save him with her magic. But the reader cannot be sure. Martin's description of Mirri's actions as she begins the ritual to save Drogo grants them an air of mystery: "Mirri Maz Duur chanted words in a tongue that Dany did not know, and a knife appeared in her hand [. . .]. It looked old; hammered red bronze, leaf-shaped, its blade covered with ancient glyphs" (*A Game of Thrones*). Something important is clearly happening here. "Once I begin to sing," the woman notes, "no one must enter this tent. My song will wake powers old and dark. The dead will dance here this night. No living man must look on them" (*A Game of Thrones*).

Mirri begins the spell with a splash of blood from Drogo's horse and essentially ends it with the blood of childbirth as Dany goes into labor. However, Dany's son is stillborn and monstrous. Drogo survives, but he is only preserved at death's door, leaving him a husk of the man he once was.

Is Mirri's magic real? Dany believes that it is—and that Mirri used it to take revenge on Drogo and his *khalasar* for the pain they had inflicted upon her and her village. Certainly something horrific happened to Dany's child, born dead, reptilian, filled with maggots, and described as "dead for years." Following Mirri's equation of blood and sacrifice, Dany builds up Drogo's funeral pyre with his treasure, his body, the dragon eggs, and the bound Mirri Maz Duur, sentencing the woman to a fiery death. Then she, too, walks into the flames. By however such things are measured, the sacrifice is deemed a high enough price to pay to awaken the dragon eggs.

And whatever doubts Dany—and the reader—might have had about the reality of magic are swept away.

By the time *A Clash of Kings* begins, other fantastical things we've only heard about through legends begin to appear: wargs, greenseers, pyromancers. There can now be no doubt: this is a world in which magic is real, if not commonplace. The birth of Dany's dragons may seem to herald its arrival, but magic has been there all along, if only diminished or slumbering.

The Slow Boil

In an April 2011 interview with the *New York Times*, Martin described the process of adding magic to his story as akin to turning up the fire underneath a crab in a pot: "You put a crab in hot water, he'll jump right out. But you put him in cold water and you gradually heat it up—the hot water is fantasy and magic, and the crab is the audience."

From the beginning of A Song of Ice and Fire, Martin broadcasts the existence of magic in the world. By opening with the Others, he shows us that there are supernatural monsters that prowl the night, forcing us to ask ourselves: What else might be out there? But by keeping the fantastic rare and mysterious, he also allows us to be surprised when we encounter it—and allows the reader who does not usually enjoy fantasy to become swept up in the story.

This slow boil, this insistence on mystery, does more than that, however. It lends the magic a greater sense of importance and power. It also keeps both characters and readers guessing as to the true nature of magic in the world. The aura of mystery heightens the sense that magic is dangerous, though in this case, that's not just an illusion. Magic comes at a high price. It is dangerous, often incredibly so.

When Dany asks her to save Drogo, for example, Mirri warns that the spell will have a high cost and require a great sacrifice. This is not something to be bargained for with gold or horseflesh, though it will be paid with that, too. Mirri tells us, "Only death may pay for life" (*A Game of Thrones*). Though the *maegi*'s bloodmagic has tragic results, it teaches Dany, and us, the most essential rules of magic in the series: it cannot be handled easily and always demands a high price.

The Red Comet

A Clash of Kings opens with another strong omen: the terrible red comet blazing across the sky. Unlike the stag and the direwolf, though, this event is much harder to interpret and most characters see what they want in it. King Joffrey sees the comet as a blessing of Lannister crimson; Edmure Tully sees Tully red and a sign of victory; Greatjon Umber sees a symbol of vengeance; Brynden Tully, Aeron Greyjoy, and Osha all see it as a portent of war and bloodshed; and to near-blind Old Nan, who claims she can smell it, the red comet means the coming of dragons. In a sense, what the fire portends to the reader is R'hllor, the Lord of Light, and his priestess, Melisandre.

Melisandre is one of the most adept magic-wielding characters in A Song of Ice and Fire. Previously, the only red priest of R'hllor we had seen was Thoros, who was more caricature than commanding; although a master of the tournaments with his flaming sword, he was bald, fat, and often drunk. Melisandre, in contrast, is sexy, sophisticated, and introduced in a scene where the stakes are life and death. Stannis Baratheon's ancient maester, Cressen, is convinced Melisandre is a toxic influence on Stannis, so he tries to poison her. But Melisandre claims to have seen his feeble attempt in her fires and warns him that she knows his plot. When Cressen refuses to turn from his path, both drink from the poisoned wine, but only Cressen is killed. Melisandre's sorcery keeps her safe.

In many ways, Melisandre is the embodiment of the lesson Dany learns—that magic comes at a tremendous cost. We are often not privy to how Melisandre is "paying" for her sorceries, but what we do learn indicates the payments are steep.

Melisandre has convinced Stannis that his path to kingship leads through the fires of R'hllor, that he is the legendary hero Azor Ahai, reborn, destined to wield the fabled sword

Lightbringer and unite and protect Westeros from the Great Other. Whether Stannis himself believes that or not—and much evidence suggests that Melisandre is flat-out wrong here, despite her demonstrable power—he listens to her counsel, trusts her implicitly, and, if he is not a full convert to her religion, is willing to feed pretty much anything she suggests into the fire. To recreate Lightbringer, Stannis symbolically sacrifices idols of his old faith, the Seven, in a great bonfire, and then draws the blade out of the burning form of the Mother.

However, Stannis does not seem to have given up enough to create a new blade: his first weapon is a charred ruin, the second blazes with light but no heat. (It is unclear if he made another attempt, or if Melisandre just put a glamor on the burned blade.) The myths of Azor Ahai say that he ruined two swords in the making. The first he tempered in water after working thirty days and nights at the forge, and it shattered. The second took fifty days and nights, was plunged into the heart of a lion to cool, and still it broke. The third attempt took one hundred days and nights; he summoned his wife and asked her to bare her breast. He tempered it in her heart—the steepest of sacrifices—and her soul combined with the sword to make Lightbringer, the Red Sword of Heroes, used to defeat the Others during the Long Night.

Melisandre is constantly feeding sacrifices to her ever-hungry fires. It is said she burns a man to give Stannis fair winds for his ships. She places leeches on Edric Storm, bastard son of King Robert, and tosses the blood-engorged worms into the flames while reciting the names of Stannis's foes—Joffrey, Balon, and Robb—to bring them to destruction (and soon enough, all three perish in terrible ways). She asks for more than a taste of Edric's blood; there is power in royal blood, she says, power enough to wake a stone dragon, and she wants to feed him to the flames. Although Stannis relents, Davos had foreseen the danger and smuggled Edric away beyond their reach. Later, she asks to sacrifice the King-Beyond-the-Wall's son, as well, though she is similarly thwarted by Jon Snow.

For many readers, it is not an image of fire but of shadow that represents Melisandre: First, the shadow of Stannis that crept into Renly's tent and assassinated him—a shadow with the power to slice through his gorget and cut his throat. Second, the shadow Davos witnesses when he rows Melisandre underneath the walls of Storm's End. Like the Wall, this ancient castle was built with powerful protective wards and her spells cannot cross the barrier. As soon as they pass under the walls, Melisandre is suddenly nine months pregnant and giving birth to a shadow; it crawls forth, as tall as a man, with Stannis's profile.

These spells, too, come at a great cost, though the sacrifice again is not Melisandre's. She draws the power for these shadow spells directly from Stannis, making him look years older and haggard and filling his sleep with nightmares.

Melisandre is not the only agent of the Lord of Light, and hers is not the only magic we see done in his name. When Thoros gives the fallen Lord Beric Dondarrion the "last kiss," a standard ritual of fire, it brings Lord Beric back from the dead, surprising them both. Thoros restores Lord Beric's life six times, but each attempt is harder and causes Lord Beric to lose—to sacrifice—a bit more of his self. After the last incident, he can no longer remember his castle, his betrothed, his favorite foods, and more. Rather than go on and continually diminish, Lord Beric passes the flame of rebirth to Lady Catelyn, restoring her as Lady Stoneheart, but this is no favor. Rather than lessen the stakes, the notion of resurrection is more like a fate worse than death.

Most recently, *A Dance with Dragons* has introduced us to Moqorro, the Black Flame, who is fished out of the sea and joins the service of Victarion Greyjoy, claiming Greyjoy has the support of the Lord of Light. Like Thoros and Melisandre, this red priest has power; he heals Victarion's putrid hand and sacrifices Maester Kerwin to bring the ship good winds. And he can read the Valyrian glyphs on the Dragon Horn.

This artifact—another magical horn the legends speak of—was discovered by Euron Greyjoy, reportedly in the ruins of Valyria, and when blown it sounds like a thousand screaming souls. Cragorn, Euron's man, collapsed with blisters on his lips after he blew it. When he died, a short time later, his lungs were charred black as soot. Moqorro tells Victarion that the horn will bind dragons, but any who sound it will die. The horn must be claimed with blood—only death may pay for life, or power, as it were.

A Game of Magic

The magic in A Song of Ice and Fire is so effective and so fascinating in the story because it always comes with a cost. But that cost itself—the rules of the game of magic—are difficult for us as readers to decipher. Even knowing what elements can precisely be called "magic" is tricky to ascertain.

When we were designing the pen-and-paper roleplaying game *A Game of Thrones d20*, we wrestled with the question of how to define magic. RPGs traditionally codify these kinds of abilities for players and antagonists to use, but we settled on a story-based approach, after talking more about theme and feeling than mechanics. This actually upset some players, who wanted a system that was more rigid, like the one used in *Dungeons & Dragons*, where every character can do specific, codified spells at a specific level. But that struck me as completely against the spirit of A Song of Ice and Fire. Instead, we decided that any character could learn a spell as long as he or she had a sufficiently high Wisdom, enough ranks in Knowledge of Arcana, and had a background trait that felt right (like Dreams, Blood of the Dragon, or Blood of the First Men). But even those who did not have formal training might create a magical working. As we stated it in the rules: "in rare circumstances, a combination of determination, fate, and luck can allow a character to spontaneously create a magical effect. Such effects are not brought about by casual attempts at magical working. Instead, they require the sort of talent derived from temporary madness."

I think it safe to say we got at least the spirit right. The latest roleplaying game based on the series—*A Song of Ice and Fire Roleplaying*, from Green Ronin Publishing—also takes a minimalist approach. In chats I've had with the games developers, Chris Pramas and Joseph D. Carriker, it's clear their focus is more on *what* magic does, and what it costs, than *how* it does it.

That mirrors the way magic works in the novels. Martin has left the rules of magic in A Song of Ice and Fire intentionally ambiguous. In the end, it doesn't really matter if wargs, red priests, and Targaryens are "dipping" into the same pool to power their enchantments or not, or doing so in the same way, as long as the author knows the rules and keeps them consistent. And keeps the use of magic restrained. "To have an epic fantasy, you need some magic," Martin also noted in that *New York Times* interview. "But I believe in judicious use of magic."

There is no doubt that magic is integral to the spirit of A Song of Ice and Fire. I think we wouldn't enjoy the story half so much without the dragons. As Martin wrote in "On Fantasy," "We read fantasy to find the colors again, I think. To taste strong spices and hear the songs the sirens sang."

With scores of chapters and hundreds of pages still to go in the series, it is clear that the rising forces of magic will shape the future of Westeros. The trick for the author and characters both is to manipulate the magic without letting it consume them. For the denizens of Westeros, the threat inherent in magic's use is a gruesome death or, like Catelyn Stark, a fate worse than death. For its creator, the threat is more profound—having his stark and original setting become just another predictable abode of lightning-hurling wizards and city-scorching flying lizards.

Perhaps the words of the Horned Lord, a former King-Beyond-the-Wall, from *A Storm of Swords* say it best: "[S]orcery is a sword without a hilt. There is no safe way to grasp it."

◆ ◆ ◆

JESSE SCOBLE is, in no particular order, a writer, game designer, and story editor. He has won awards, written a Western horror script, and contributed to more than thirty RPG books and related anthologies. He was Creative Director on the RPG *A Game of Thrones d20*, and also helped out on the more recent *A Song of Ice and Fire Roleplaying*. He worked on NCsoft's *City of Heroes*, Ganz's *Webkinz* and *Tail Towns*, multiple Ubisoft projects, and the *Marvel Heroic RPG* from Margaret Weis Productions. A Canadian by blood, he relocated to Austin in the scorching year of 2011, to work as Senior Content Designer (read: writer) on *Wizard101* for KingsIsle. He has two small children, A (3.3) and AD (0.3), who are already being indoctrinated into the wonders of fantasy and games. He makes a mean mojito.

PETYR BAELISH AND THE MASK OF SANITY

THE WORLD OF A Song of Ice and Fire is an unbelievably cruel place: Heroes fall to the blade with no regard for the nobility of their character or the righteousness of their cause. Villains live on with seemingly little comeuppance for their wickedness. Life is hard, and the gods, old or new, are deaf to the cries of nobles and smallfolk alike. In such a world only those who can harden themselves to the suffering of those around them stand a chance of winning the game of thrones.

The bonds of family, faith, and fealty can prevent most people from ever achieving the state of callousness needed to claim victory, but Petyr "Littlefinger" Baelish isn't a normal person: he is a psychopath, and this makes him an unsettlingly skilled player in the game. Littlefinger has no emotional chinks in his armor, mostly because he doesn't have any real emotions—at least in the way that normal people understand them. Without any of the emotional vulnerabilities of a relatively healthy human being, Littlefinger is insulated against the pitfalls that await others who fight for power in Westeros. All of those who seek to best him share one fatal mistake: they assume that Littlefinger operates by the same rules that they do. They soon learn otherwise. Could he win the game of thrones? Quite possibly, and if so, his cruelty could rival that of Aerys II.

Most people are familiar with the word "psychopath." Popular entertainment and news reporters alike love to describe murderers as "psychopathic," thinking that it simply means they're "crazy," or that the crimes they've committed are especially gruesome. People use the word "psycho" when they're talking about unpredictable or bizarre behavior, using it as a one-size-fits-all synonym for "crazy." An excellent, and amusing, example of this kind of confusion can be seen in the 1981 comedy *Stripes*. New recruit Francis Soyer attempts to intimidate the other soldiers in his unit by telling them that people call him "Psycho," and proceeds to threaten to kill them if they touch him or his stuff. The erratic, jittery Soyer is a weirdo, to be sure, but is he a psychopath? Not likely.

Psychopathy is a personality disorder, a kind of psychiatric illness that is firmly enmeshed in a person's identity. Personality disorders are usually diagnosed through a careful examination of a subject's history and, normally, a battery of psychological tests. Psychiatrists and other mental health practitioners look for specific patterns of behavior upon which to base their diagnoses. The reality of psychopathy is far removed from the grab bag of erratic and disorganized behavior the public has ascribed to the word. It isn't marked by the kind of over-the-top, twitchy excitability and aggressiveness demonstrated by the character in *Stripes*. It's actually much more subtle and disturbing.

In 1941, psychiatrist Hervey Cleckley wrote a book called *The Mask of Sanity*, a groundbreaking study that hypothesized that psychopaths possess no capacity to experience real emotions. They wear a psychological "mask" to hide their abnormality. Cleckley's book included a list of sixteen characteristics that he thought were typical of a psychopath. His fellow psychiatrists built upon this list, using parts of it to form the criteria for antisocial personality disorder, as psychopathy is known in the *Diagnostic and Statistical Manual of Mental Disorders*, a kind of bible for the profession.

There's no universally accepted criteria for identifying psychopathy, but four basic qualities are common to just about every definition: a history of engaging in criminal behavior, little to no empathy for victims, the inability to form strong emotional attachments, and a lack of sincere remorse for one's actions. Theses are the indicators we'll be looking for as we analyze Littlefinger.

Psychopaths have a history of committing acts that would be considered criminal or at least immoral by the standards of their society. Littlefinger has committed, or arranged, several murders, as the most expedient means to accruing power and wealth. All these murders are carried out in cold blood.

Littlefinger's first documented murder conspiracy sparks the War of the Five Kings, although it is not often credited as such a monumental accomplishment. Lysa Arryn poisons her husband Jon at Littlefinger's behest. Had this not occurred, Eddard Stark would have never traveled to King's Landing to become the King's Hand to Robert Baratheon. In turn, he would not have been imprisoned and executed, and the Young Wolf, Robb Stark, would not have raised his banners against King's Landing.

Littlefinger's next victim is Eddard Stark. He manipulates Stark from the moment of his arrival in King's Landing, feigning friendship until the Lord of Winterfell takes him into his confidence. Once this occurs, Littlefinger betrays Eddard's trust, leading to his capture and execution for treason. With Eddard out of the way, Littlefinger marries the conveniently widowed Lysa. The half-mad woman is ecstatic to wed her childhood love, though he murders her not long after.

At Littlefinger's behest, Dontos Hollard, the former knight and later jester in the court of King Joffrey, helps Sansa Stark escape from her forced marriage to Tyrion Lannister. After successfully accompanying Sansa to the ship that will take her from King's Landing, Littlefinger murders him. Dontos could have lived on in exile, but a blade and burial at sea are more reliable methods of ensuring he will never reveal how Sansa escaped King's Landing and with whom she left.

Littlefinger is a murderer, but A Song of Ice and Fire is full of violent men and women. What makes Littlefinger's murders so different from those committed by the other characters? Motive. Littlefinger cares only for himself, and murders entirely for his own benefit. Other characters in A Song of Ice and Fire commit murder, but they are usually motivated to do so by emotions like love, shame, or anger, in response to a potential threat, or in service to an ideological cause that they perceive to be greater than themselves. That cause isn't always noble or sensible, but motives beyond personal gain—or at least concurrent with it— are often what trigger the bloodshed. Queen Cersei may be a schemer and murderer, but she's also a mother who will do anything and everything she must in order to protect her children. Her brother Jaime flings Bran Stark from a window, but it is to protect their illicit love affair. Their youngest brother, Tyrion, arguably one of the most ethical characters in the saga, arranges the murder of the musician Symon Silver Tongue in response to his ill-considered attempt at blackmail. Even Lord Walder Frey orchestrates the events of the infamous Red Wedding partially in response to a perceived insult to his house.

Littlefinger isn't motivated by emotion. He claims to love Catelyn Stark, but his actions betray the facile declarations of his affection. Where is Littlefinger in her time of greatest need? Seducing her daughter and murdering her sister, in short order.

Lack of remorse or empathy are also hallmarks of the psychopath. Littlefinger offers cold comfort to Sansa Stark following the death of her father, telling her that he was a "piece" and not a "player" in the game. Respect for the feelings of others does not factor into his strategies. If anything, it is only considered a vulnerability to be exploited. He says as much in the same conversation with Sansa, as she poses as his daughter Alayne: "Everyone wants something, Alayne. And when you know what a man wants you know who he is, and how to move him" (*A Storm of Swords*).

Littlefinger's skill at manipulating others might only be bested by Varys's. What differentiates Littlefinger from the

Spider, though, is motive. Varys acts to preserve the stability of the kingdom. His peers may consider him untrustworthy, and he may very well be, but it is because his allegiance is to crown and country rather than any particular individual. Littlefinger's allegiance is to Littlefinger.

It is difficult to understand what it must be like to be without empathy or remorse. Human beings constantly anthropomorphize animals, despite their clearly nonhuman status. We project emotional states like hate, love, or anger on to beings incapable of feeling them in the same way we do. It is hard enough to view our relationships with our pets in an objective manner, so you can imagine how difficult it can be to conceive of, and anticipate, the actions of a human being with the emotional depth and capacity for remorse of a rattlesnake. Most people simply aren't capable of it. Then again, most people aren't Tyrion Lannister.

It should hardly come as any surprise that an astute judge of character like Tyrion has managed to see through Littlefinger's façade of normalcy. Perhaps the distance granted him as an outsider has given him a sense of perspective not easily attainable by the rest of the characters.

In *A Game of Thrones*, Tyrion offers this comment to Cersei: "Why does a bear shit in the woods? [. . .] Because it is his nature. Lying comes as easily as breathing to a man like Littlefinger. You ought to know that, you of all people." And later in the same book he sums up the Master of Coin with a single, devastating sentence: "Littlefinger has never loved anyone but Littlefinger."

Manipulation is another key quality of the psychopath. Littlefinger has no friends, only tools and playthings to be disposed of the moment they no longer suit his purposes. His favorite method of disposal is to be found at the end of a blade. He excels at this. It's a kind of genius, really: moving and shifting friends and foe alike like chess pieces upon a great board. Eddard thought that he could trust Littlefinger. So did Lysa Arryn and Ser Dontos. Sansa Stark seems to trust Littlefinger, and already she suffers for it.

Were it not for Littlefinger's Svengali-esque talent for seduction, Sansa might have already revealed her noble identity to House Royce, and ultimately the true circumstances of her aunt's death. In the light of such knowledge, Littlefinger's claim over the Eyrie and Riverlands would be tenuous at best. The lords of the Vale already despise the man, and a charge of murder could be reason enough for a hanging. For now, Sansa maintains her alias as Alayne Stone and Littlefinger remains Lord Protector.

Obviously, Littlefinger plans to once again expand his dominion. There is the matter of his ward Robert Arryn, but given the history of others who have stood in the way of Littlefinger's ambitions, the odds of the little Lord Robert reaching the age of majority are slim. Sansa's odds aren't much better. With the eldest Stark daughter out of the way, Littlefinger would be free to claim the North.

As for the superficial charm of the psychopath, nothing could describe Littlefinger better. He may seem pleasant enough—charismatic, even—but it is all a façade. Every bit of affection he shows others is in service to his personal benefit. Yes, he fought a duel for Catelyn's hand, but marrying her would have greatly improved his social standing. It's quite reasonable, given his later actions, to look back on even his earliest proclamations of love with a jaundiced eye.

Aside from the obvious answer of "power," why does Littlefinger do the things that he does? Psychopaths act because they feel entitled. They feel nothing for other people, and are often highly narcissistic. The Hare Psychopathy Checklist, a diagnostic test used to identify psychopaths, lists both "aggressive narcissism" and "grandiose self worth" as personality factors common among psychopaths. Such a combination is potentially explosive. People, and laws, stand in the way of things that the psychopath thinks he deserves. The decision to eliminate or circumvent these obstacles can be an easy choice, especially if the likelihood that he will be caught is little or nonexistent. A pre-industrial society like Westeros would be an ideal environment for an intelligent psychopath, especially one whose noble status would lend some protection against common law.

One of the great charms of Martin's epic is that the author avoids the good versus evil dichotomy present in much of fantasy fiction, instead opting to present a more textured, realistic human tableau. Just exactly who the heroes and villains are depends on one's perspective, and even then neither designation is necessarily static: the despised monster of one book may be the hero of another, or vice versa. Kind men and women can become corrupted, slipping from the moral high ground inch by inch. Sometimes they pick themselves up again, and sometimes they don't. Conversely, the most callous of characters may learn from their experiences and sometimes in spite of themselves feel pity or even respect for their enemies. Can we really say any of these things for Littlefinger? No, I don't think that we can. His affections are feigned, as is his sympathy. There is nothing inside of him that can be recognized as compassion. There is no potential for growth because, metaphorically speaking, he is dead inside. Littlefinger hides the nihilistic vacuity of his inner being behind Cleckley's mask of sanity. He is a monster among men.

Martin's saga is often compared to J.R.R. Tolkien's The Lord of the Rings, but with all due respect to Professor Tolkien and his wonderful work, the psychological complexity just isn't there. With the exception of Boromir, Aragorn and company are "good" in a way that is rarely encountered outside of fiction. The One Ring corrupts good men. It is clearly a supernatural source of evil in a world where people (and elves, dwarves, and hobbits) are essentially good. Martin doesn't introduce an external source of evil in his work because it isn't required. There is corruption and depravity and sin in A Song of Ice and Fire, but it can all be ascribed to human fallibility. Supernatural evil is exceptionally rare, and when it appears, it is almost uniformly alien. There's nothing seductive about the white walkers and their wights. They don't communicate by any other means than bloodshed, and offer nothing more than the oblivion of undeath.

A supernatural conception of evil provides an easy out for readers who might otherwise look at a character's desperately cruel actions and question whether they themselves may be capable of the same given the right circumstances. Where there's a darkly seductive magic ring—or, to consider the real world, a horned man holding a pitchfork—luring the righteous off the path of the just, we can continue to cleave to the illusion that evil is something outside of us instead of existing as a potential within us all. Martin's saga offers no such comfort. Evil in Martin's books usually wears a very human face, and most often that face is one that is not all that far removed from our own.

The fact that Littlefinger wears a mask of normalcy makes him even more frightening than the white walkers, wights, or petty sadists of Westeros. The Bloody Mummers advertise their depravity, and Gregor Clegane's unhinged rage guarantees him a wide berth. Ser Jaime Lannister probably won't cut you down without some reason, minor though it may be. Littlefinger, with his good upbringing, neat appearance, and friendly smile seems like someone you should be able to trust with your secrets, even your life. To do so is to risk forfeiture of both, but it is likely that you won't realize the danger until you feel the blade biting deeply into your throat or the hand on your back as you stumble out the high tower window.

Could Littlefinger ever find some manner of redemption? Unlikely. Iniquity, subterfuge, and violence have defined his character in the saga, and a Littlefinger suddenly gone "good" would not be Littlefinger. Psychopathy is for life, and Martin's commitment to psychological realism would probably not allow for such an unlikely turnabout.

A Song of Ice and Fire is not known for its storybook endings, but this is part of what makes the books so entertaining. Good is not always rewarded, nor evil always punished. As a matter of fact, sometimes it seems that evil often escapes punishment. In other words, Westeros is very much a world like our own. Few of us play a game of thrones. Most of us are limited to, at most, a game of cubicles. But there are heroes and villains among us, and some days we can play both roles. We also have our own Littlefingers. Some lurk in dark alleys with axes, while others siphon away our pensions and turn our government against us. Some of them are as close as the apartment next door, or perhaps even the nearest mirror.

If they wear the mask of sanity as well as Littlefinger, though, we'll have a hard time recognizing them, until it's far too late.

◆ ◆ ◆

MATT STAGGS is a former mental health worker and journalist now employed as a book publicist, author, and podcaster. Matt is a regular contributor of reviews, interviews, and feature articles at Suvudu, publisher Random House's official science fiction and fantasy website. He is also the host of the DisinfoCast, the official podcast of the Disinformation Company. In his increasingly limited spare time, Matt enjoys drawing, playing tabletop roleplaying games, arguing about movies, and researching topics in psychology, culture, religion, folklore, and Forteana. He lives in central Mississippi with his wife, two cats, dog, and bearded dragon, Smaug. Should you wish to do so, you can find Matt on Twitter at @mattstaggs, Facebook at facebook.com/mattstaggs, and at his shamefully neglected website mattstaggs.com.

◆ BRENT HARTINGER ◆

A DIFFERENT KIND OF OTHER

*The Role of Freaks and Outcasts
in A Song of Ice and Fire*

WHO DOESN'T LOVE AN underdog?

As humans, most of us seem to be instinctively drawn to outsiders, to the excluded. At least on some level, most of us sympathize with those who are denied even the *opportunity* to prove their full worth. We recognize that's just not fair.

Writers know that audiences love underdog stories. From *Rocky* to *Rudy*, *Star Wars* to *Seabiscuit*, people never seem to tire of them. Besides, if the antagonist isn't stronger than the protagonist, at least at first, there *is* no story.

But there are outsiders and then there are outsiders. The sprawling cast of George R.R. Martin's A Song of Ice and Fire series includes a surprisingly large number of major characters who are considered social rejects, if not outright freaks, by the people around them: gender-nonconformists like Arya, Brienne, and Varys; at least two disabled characters, Bran and Donal; the overweight Samwell; Jon, a bastard; a number of gay men, including Renly and Loras.

And, of course, the series includes a dwarf, Tyrion: not the beard-wearing, underground-dwelling race of German mythology (and many other works of fantasy), but an actual genetic dwarf.

Indeed, of the series' fourteen major point-of-view characters to date—Tyrion, Arya, Jon, Daenerys, Bran, Samwell, Brienne, Catelyn, Jaime, Cersei, Eddard, Davos, Theon, and Sansa—at least the first seven violate major gender or social norms. Until just the last few decades, individuals such as these have typically been treated as objects of scorn, ridicule, or pity—not just in most literature, but in the Western civilization that this literature has reflected. When these outsiders haven't been stereotyped, they've been ignored.

It's hard to say which is the deeper cut.

Women, meanwhile, have often been prescribed equally narrow roles in both life and literature: almost always defined by their relationship to a man. Like most women in history, Ice and Fire's females might be considered outsiders by mere virtue of their gender. Even as a future queen, Sansa, for example, is completely powerless over her destiny.

A Song of Ice and Fire is set in a quasi-medieval setting where prejudices about these and other minorities couldn't be much more brutal or bigoted. But the sensibility of the series is decidedly modern. Outsiders are *not* stereotyped or ignored. On the contrary, these characters are brought front and center, their perspectives presented as no less important than those of the more traditional ones.

In fact, maybe they're *more* important. In the series, the experience of being a freak or a misfit seems to make a person more sensitive to the plight of others, and more heroic—or at least as "heroic" as one can be in the brutal, complicated lands of Westeros and Essos. Meanwhile, other characters start out as "insiders," but end up as outsiders. The transition often changes their perspectives for the better.

Together, ice and fire make steam, and in George R.R. Martin's masterwork, it's mostly the freaks and outcasts who get burned. But that doesn't mean they don't have something very important to say about it.

◆ ◆ ◆

It's not like the fantasy genre hasn't long had its share of outsiders.

In fact, you could argue that the whole genre is built on a very specific kind of "outsider": the dispossessed king or exiled prince determined to reclaim his throne. From Odysseus and Rama to modern-day characters like Luke Skywalker, Harry Potter, and Tarzan, they may start the story as outsiders, but they have greatness in their blood, and their rightful "throne" is just waiting for them to rise up and seize it.

Other famous fantasy outsiders may not be of actual royal blood, but they're called to greatness anyway, compelled to complete some important quest to which they and they alone are uniquely suited. Only Frodo has the pureness of heart to handle the One Ring without succumbing to its darker temptations. And while the Pevensie children may seem at first glance to be unlikely heroes, they're literally summoned by Aslan for greatness nonetheless—and they're fulfilling ancient prophecies to boot.

The journey of the traditional fantasy hero is all spelled out in Joseph Campbell's landmark exploration of myths, *The Hero with a Thousand Faces* (1949): first, a "call to greatness," then a consultation with a mentor, a Merlin or a Gandalf, who explains the quest ahead. Typically, all these fantasy "outsiders" also end up with a ragtag but stalwart band of other pseudo-misfits to help them achieve their destiny.

Let's not forget all the useful magic items these heroes are also granted: rings of power or swords of destiny. Michael Moorcock's Elric of Melniboné is but a frail, albino prince—at least until the magic sword Stormbringer transforms him into a mighty warrior (albeit at a heavy cost). And no matter which legend you believe as to how King Arthur comes to possess the sword Excalibur—whether he pulls it from a stone or receives it from the Lady of the Lake—both versions unequivocally declare him to be the choice of the gods to rule England.

But just how much are these characters really outsiders? Sure, these boys and men of privilege have usually lost some of their standing in the world, and they learn valuable lessons by trying to get it back. That said, they're still almost always boys and men of privilege.

This paradigm made sense in its time. After all, most of these tropes date from a pre-Enlightenment era when attitudes about minorities and outsiders were so entrenched that it was difficult to even *conceive* of a hero as anyone other than a boy or man of privilege. It was just *obvious* that big problems could only be solved by just such a person. And let's face it: it was men of privilege who were invariably financing and disseminating these stories, too.

Still, if the protagonists in these tales are outsiders at all, it's usually only due to circumstances, not as a result of anything innate about them. Meanwhile, the perspectives of *true* outcasts, those who were considered freaks and outcasts by their actual nature, were ignored. Ironically, they were excluded even from the story of the outcast.

Basically, few authors bothered to ask a very obvious question: if the hero has a thousand faces, why are almost all of those faces male? And straight? And of average height? And of average weight? And why do they always follow the accepted gender norms?

Times have changed. George R.R. Martin isn't the first contemporary author to ask questions about exactly who should be front and center in the story, not by a long shot. A significant portion of late-twentieth-century fiction is devoted to exploring the perspective of the outsider by nature, the "other." Yet even today, popular entertainment focuses overwhelmingly on the slender, the heterosexual, the average-heighted, the conventionally-abled, and the traditionally gendered. This is even truer in the fantasy genre, which has only very recently started seriously exploring stories beyond the one about the exiled prince or the Chosen One seeking to claim his legacy.

Despite their "outsider" sensibility, or maybe *because* of it, the books in the Song of Ice and Fire series have found mainstream success in a way that few such fantasy projects have before.

Take Bran Stark. He's young, confident, and adventurous: a classic fantasy hero. But his bravado leads to disaster when he impetuously climbs a forgotten tower and peeks in on Jaime Lannister having incestuous sex with his sister Cersei, the queen. Determined to keep their relationship a secret, Jaime throws Bran from the window, intending to kill him, but actually only permanently disabling him.

In most fantasy epics, this would be the end of his storyline. After all, Narnia is not wheelchair accessible (neither, for that matter, is Westeros). For Martin, though, this is literally just the *beginning* of Bran's story: he is thrown off that ledge in only his second point-of-view chapter.

Then there's Samwell Tarly, who isn't called by the gods or destiny to do anything. He has no mentor stopping by to detail a task ahead and no artifacts of great power are bestowed upon him. On the contrary, in the world of Westeros, Sam is specifically excluded from "greatness" because of his body type: he's fat. He is, in fact, the eldest son in the Tarly family, but his father declares him unfit for leadership because of his lack of physical prowess and offers him a deal: renounce his inheritance and "take the black" as a member of the Night's Watch, thereby allowing his younger brother to become the family heir, or soon suffer an unfortunate "hunting accident."

Brienne of Tarth, meanwhile, *is* an exceptional warrior, capable of matching even the mighty Jamie Lancaster in combat. The Tarly family would be proud to have her—except for the fact that Brienne's great skills don't conform to what is considered acceptable for her gender. It doesn't help that she also has tra-ditionally masculine features. So she too is rejected, considered a freak by her family and treated with scorn and ridicule by almost everyone else, disparagingly called "Brienne the Beauty."

Brienne, Samwell, and Bran may all be noble-born, but there is something in their very natures, something they did not choose and cannot control, that makes each of them not quite fit for their status. They're disappointments, even freaks, to their families and cultures.

Martin sees them with a much more sympathetic eye. Indeed, their stories are so valid and interesting that he elevates them to point-of-view characters. Becoming disabled, for example, leads Bran to begin experiencing visions. By the time of *A Dance with Dragons*, Bran has even developed his skills as both a greenseer, or prophet, and a skinchanger, capable of viewing the world through the eyes of animals.

In other words, his becoming disabled *wasn't* the end of his story. On the contrary, it's the moment when his story just started to get good.

Much has been made of the shocking realism in A Song of Ice and Fire. People die prematurely and in horrible ways, women are casually raped, and everyone suffers—a lot. Things stink in Westeros, in more ways than one. But the most shocking aspect to Martin's realism may be this lavish attention he pays to the freaks and outsiders. Throughout the series, these characters matter. Their statuses grant them unique perspectives that are different from the majority, from those who are not excluded, and those perspectives prove important to both the structure of the novels and the workings of the plot.

Who is it that finally treats Brienne with kindness and is able to see beyond the limitations of his culture, recognizing her for what she is? It's Renly Baratheon, a closeted gay man secretly in love with the Knight of Flowers. Apparently his own knowledge of being a "freak" has made him more likely to understand and be sympathetic to Brienne's unjust predicament. Meanwhile, it might be Jon Snow's outcast past as Ned Stark's bastard son that helps him feel sympathy for Samwell, who is ridiculed and called "Ser Piggy" by the other members of the Night's Watch. (Just because the men of the Night's Watch are all outcasts themselves doesn't mean they can't reject others, too. On the contrary, creating social codes that play outsiders against each other has long been an important way those in power have maintained their control.)

Despite Jon's faith in him, Samwell mostly remains a hopeless warrior. Yet Sam is smart, and Jon's loyalty to him pays off when Sam cleverly manipulates the other members of the Watch into supporting his candidacy for Lord Commander.

Sometimes it pays to be nice to the freaks.

So the outcasts in A Song of Ice and Fire are all the good guys, right? They've learned important lessons from their oppression, and they live lives of quiet, stoic dignity outside the halls of power? When writing about outcast or minority characters, many authors fall into exactly this trap. But the idea of the "noble savage"—the notion that being a despised other always endows you with great dignity and wisdom—is just another stereotype. It's a well-intentioned one, but it's almost as limiting as the others. When minority or outcast characters exist in a story solely to teach lessons to members of the majority, it's just one more way of seeing everything from the majority point of view.

That said, it's the rare outsider character in A Song of Ice and Fire whose perspective is not *informed* in some way by his or her experiences as a social reject.

Varys is a fat, bald, effeminate eunuch. He's also a master of information, using his "little birds" to constantly spy on those around him, manipulating everyone, always for his own secretive ends. He'll do what needs to be done, even if it sometimes means betraying friends and allies.

But how much of Varys's paranoia and ruthlessness are the result of his own horrible powerlessness when, as a boy, he was forced to take a drug that paralyzed him—but did not shield him from pain—so he could be involuntarily castrated? Surely his perspective is also colored by the fact that as an adult, most people see him as a freak, and he knows better than anyone exactly what kind of justice a freak usually receives.

It's also debatable just how self-centered Varys really is. In the dungeons of the Red Keep, Ned asks the Master of Whisperers outright to declare his real endgame: "Peace," Varys says, and a good case can be made from his actions to date in the series that he's telling the truth.

Still, the outsider characters in Ice and Fire do not always act nobly. Their paths are usually pretty complicated. And that's exactly the point. Martin grants the freaks and outsiders the dignity of living in three dimensions.

Like Varys, Tyrion Lannister, "the Imp" even to his family, sometimes seems to have a flexible morality, frequently claiming to care for nothing and no one but himself. It's mostly just the "honorable" moral and legal codes of Westeros that he rejects—codes that always favor the powerful.

During his imprisonment in Lysa Arryn's Eyrie in *A Game of Thrones*, Tyrion staves off execution by cleverly manipulating the system of rules. He tricks Catelyn into a trial, then demands trial by combat, with the absent Jaime as his champion. This makes such a trial virtually impossible. Then, it's implied, he advises his eventual champion, Bronn, to fight in such a way that his more accomplished, but heavily armored, opponent will be at a disadvantage.

Stand and fight fair? That's the last thing Varys or Tyrion would ever do! Why would they? The rules are rigged: they're set up by and for kings and princes with well-trained, well-armored champions. Tyrion and Varys might not fight fair, but it wasn't a fair fight to begin with. If they play the game the way it's intended to be played, the outcasts always lose.

"A eunuch has no honor," Varys tells Ned. It's a luxury only non-freaks can afford.

Having suffered dearly under the rules of an unforgiving society, outcasts such as Tyrion and Varys pay keen attention to rules, precisely so they can manipulate them in order to give themselves a fighting chance. They also keep a close eye on other outsiders, as they can often be valuable allies. Despite being noble-born, Tyrion is able to convincingly speak to them as equals. It's not a coincidence that he's able to win over both the members of the ostracized hill tribes and the wildings.

When Tyrion encounters Jon Snow up at the Wall, he gives Ned's bastard son the classic, but profound, advice of the misfit: "Let [those who mock you] see that their words can cut you, and you'll never be free of their mockery. If they want to give you [an insulting] name, take it, make it your own. Then they can't hurt you with it anymore" (*A Game of Thrones*).

It seems there's a band with ties even deeper than those of the Night's Watch: the brotherhood of the outcast.

Another outcast, the one-armed Donal Noye, gives Jon a related lesson on the nature of outsiders. "They hate me because I'm better than they are," Jon complains to the smith, after his fellow recruits in the Watch react badly to his victories over them on the training grounds. Those victories are hardly a triumph worth celebrating; Jon's life of relative privilege at Winterfell has made him a better fighter than the commoners training with him.

"No," Donal responds. "They hate you because you act like you're better than they are" (*A Game of Thrones*).

Which isn't to say that the brotherhood of the outcast doesn't have its own blind spots, especially when it comes to sex and gender.

Tyrion, for example, falls in love at the age of thirteen with Tysha, a girl he and his brother Jamie had rescued from some bandits. She loves him back and they marry in secret. But when his father Tywin discovers the relationship, he cruelly commands Jamie to say that the girl is a whore who had been paid to act like she loved the Imp. Then Tywin directs his entire guard to rape the girl, even forcing Tyrion to go last. After that, Tyrion seems incapable of forging a healthy relationship and employs a long line of prostitutes to service him sexually.

The details of his sex life are humiliating, at least from Tyrion's point of view. But the fact that these details are offered up to readers is anything but. The books are granting even this outcast character the dignity of *having* a sexuality, something that has long been denied fictional dwarf characters, and fictional freaks and outcasts in general—a far greater indignity indeed.

Later, when Tyrion is made to wed Sansa, he does not force himself on her sexually, despite the clear opportunity to do so. It's hard not to conclude this decision is linked with his sexual history, not to mention his whole experience as a reviled outsider.

As bad as Tyrion's experiences are, we should remember that it is Tysha, after all, who is gang raped. And what of Tyrion's many prostitutes, who must submit to him and all men for a living? Indeed, what of the sexuality of most of the female characters in the series? Those who aren't raped outright at some point in the story must live with the knowledge that such sexual degradation always exists as a very real possibility.

One argument against such brutal content, and it's a compelling one, is that the sexual humiliation of women in A Song of Ice and Fire is just too cavalier, too omnipresent—that it overwhelms other aspects of the books. How would male readers react to an epic story written by a woman where virtually every chapter features a man being violently assaulted?

The counterargument posits that, by presenting all the raping and whoring so casually, Martin is commenting on women and powerlessness, perhaps even making an ironic point: women are the ultimate outsiders. Their complete and vicious degradation is so commonplace that almost no one in Westeros notices. For the majority of characters—including Tyrion, who usually has a keen eye for fellow outcasts, and even many of the other women in the cast—the nonstop violence against women is mostly invisible, barely even worth a mention.

This violence, of course, is true not just in Westeros and Essos: it's been true for most of real-world human history. Is it any more visible in our history books and museums?

History, they say, is written by the victors.

Not every character in the series is an outsider. Those that aren't tend to be—naturally—the queens and kings and royals who are actually ruling. Alas, most of these insiders tend to be petty, easily manipulated fools such as Lysa Arryn and even King Robert at times, or else outright tyrants such as Aerys, Cersei, Joffrey, and Tywin. And woe to the world if Viserys Targaryen, Daenerys's brother, was to ever actually become king!

Other insiders become outsiders over the course of the story—not necessarily as a result of anything in their fundamental natures, but more due to changing circumstances. These are the more traditional fantasy outcast storylines in A Song of Ice and Fire, but they're still worth examining.

Daenerys may be a de facto outsider by virtue of her gender, and another kind of outsider as a result of her race and nationality relative to the people she's trying to lead, but she's still a person of privilege. In fact, despite her gender, hers may be the books' most classic fantasy storyline: a royal in exile seeking to reclaim her thrown who is given the benefit of several mentors and a magic item, in the form of three dragon's eggs. Whether her destiny is real or not, she certainly *believes* it is, so much so that she is impervious to fire.

Daenerys begins the Ice and Fire saga as a timid thirteen-year-old girl, totally dependent on her older brother. The experience of their exile to Essos—her becoming an actual outcast—changes her. She rises to the occasion, but Viserys does not. Her entire series-long story arc is that of someone who has seen her world taken away, but then slowly begins to rebuild that world into something far greater than what existed before. In the process, Daenerys is utterly transformed. For her, the experience of being cast out literally builds her character, makes her strong in ways she never could have imagined before. It's the traditional fantasy outcast's ultimate triumph.

Even Jaime Lannister finds himself with a new perspective when he becomes an outcast of sorts after losing a hand to Vargo Hoat. First, he falls into a deep depression and loses the will to live. Eventually Brienne talks him out of his hopelessness; Jaime is so moved by this that he later rescues her from Vargo, and then saves her again from death at the hand of Loras Tyrell. When he is finally reunited with Cersei, he quickly realizes how much he has changed and that their relationship is irrevocably doomed. His perspectives have shifted so much that he even confesses an unforgivable sin to Tyrion: that he was lying when he said the woman Tyrion once loved did not love him back.

Lose your hand, gain some character. It's a direct correlation.

◆ ◆ ◆

Here's what we know about the world of A Song of Ice and Fire: the pampered, entitled experience of most of the royals leads to moral disaster. The political system may say otherwise, but we, the reader, know these folks are not fit to rule, no matter their genes, their gold, or their armies.

Here's what else we know: those characters who are outcasts as a result of something in their fundamental nature tend to be more sensitive to the plight of others, especially other outsiders. Just as in the real world, it's never black-and-white, but all things being equal, it's good to have Jon Snow at your back, and you'll probably have better luck with Tyrion than the other Lannisters.

Basically, freaks and outcasts tend to be well worth knowing. Even those noble characters who become outcasts due more to circumstances than their natures tend to gain perspectives on the world that make them stronger. In other words, the woman with the pet dragons just might be worth following, and it's definitely better to be stuck with Jaime Lannister after he loses a hand than before.

After five books, it seems pretty clear that no one ever wins the game of thrones, at least not for long. But when it comes to being a better person, it might not be such a bad thing to be cast out of the castle completely.

◆ ◆ ◆

BRENT HARTINGER is the author of many books, mostly for teenagers, including the gay teen novel *Geography Club* (soon to be a motion picture) and its four sequels. His other books include *Shadow Walkers*, a paranormal romance, and the forthcoming *Three Truths and a Lie*, a psychological thriller. Visit Brent online at brenthartinger.com.

◆ CAROLINE SPECTOR ◆

POWER AND FEMINISM IN WESTEROS

THE USE AND ABUSE of power is the one constant theme of George R.R. Martin's A Song of Ice and Fire. Power, large or small, inevitably corrupts in Westeros, no matter who wields it and no matter the righteousness of their cause. Even as the disenfranchised women of Westeros seize the autonomy they need for power, once they begin taking it, they inevitably fall prey to the same potentially corrupting influences the men experience.

Feminism is, at its heart, about the empowerment of women. This power takes the form of both political power (e.g., suffrage) and personal power. Holding power in the political realm allows women the same influence in society men have. Personal power affords women their own agency to make choices for themselves regarding their lives, whether it's whom they marry, the ability to consent to sex, the right to choose a profession, or just the right to choose the life they wish to live without being coerced by others.

Both men and women are oppressed by the existing power structure in Westeros. This is especially true for characters failing to conform to the prevailing gender standards, such as Brienne, a "masculine" woman; Varys, a "feminine" man; Samwell Tarly, a man who confounds his masculine role by being gentle and kind; and Asha Greyjoy, a woman who is a powerful leader of men. But it is the women who are most obviously in need of their own agency. This is not to say that women don't have power, but by and large, their avenues to power are circumscribed. Asha, for example, commands a remarkable amount of respect for a woman in Westeros, but not enough for the men to rally around her to take the Seastone Chair, though she's by far the best choice to do so. And outright rule by women is an almost unheard of event. Daenerys Targaryen is remarkable and dangerous in every sense because her very existence is perilous to the current power structure.

Critics of the series point to examples of sexual assault in the books, the lack of women in positions of power, and the trappings of traditional medieval fantasy as indicative of a lack of feminist perspective in the narrative. This analysis suffers from the notion that an author writing about a thing—for example, rape—somehow suggests he or she condones it or is simply exploiting the subject matter. This makes for a shallow and facile examination of the text, taking examples out of context and failing to look at the broader scope of the work.

Confounding Expectations

Throughout A Song of Ice and Fire, Martin establishes conventional medieval fantasy tropes and then destroys them, often by revealing the corrupting influences at their heart. If the usual image of the knight is a man of courage and valor, Martin subverts that image with brutes like Sandor Clegane. If women are supposed to be virtuous, pure, and helpless, then the reader is presented with Cersei Lannister. Indeed, while Cersei functions in some ways as the traditional "Evil Queen," she is more than that easy trope. As the series progresses, it becomes clear that she is trapped by the expectations of her society, and that she lacks the ability to see how her personal and ethical shortcomings hamstring her quest for power and respect. She's wicked and pathetic at the same time.

In epic fantasy, there has to be a monumental struggle of some sort. Usually this consists of a grand, sweeping conflict between forces of good and evil that imperils the entire world, or at least the safe and civilized parts of it. In A Song of Ice and Fire, the threat to civilization is reflected in the Stark motto: "Winter Is Coming." Winter in Westeros is a multi-year affair that not only blots out the natural progression of seasons, but also brings supernatural menace from beyond the Wall. This phrase hangs over Westeros like a death sentence. It promises a threat that would, were this a traditional fantasy tale, require the courtly knights to rally, rout the obvious agents of evil, and prevent the destruction of the peaceful shire or duchy that serves as the symbolic heart of the idyllic, morally upright kingdom.

But Westeros, and the lands surrounding it, are anything but idyllic. Martin constantly throws a harsh light on the cracks in his world's culture, the moral failings of its leaders, and the deceptions at the heart of its most cherished institutions. The supposedly noble Night's Watch is populated by rapists. The heirs to the throne are the children of adulterous incest. The legends of heroic men protecting helpless women turn out to be lies and, worse, propaganda intended to encourage women to embrace their helplessness.

In fact, the tribulations of the female characters in particular play a central role in illustrating the disconnect between the society's illusions about itself and the harrowing reality.

Sansa Stark: The Good Girl

As *A Game of Thrones* opens, Sansa seems an exemplar of womanly virtues, as the Westerosi elite defines them. She's docile, pretty, excels at needlepoint, and revels in the privileges afforded her by her position as Lord Eddard Stark's daughter. In short, she's royalty—and insufferable. Priggish and superior, she annoys, and is annoyed by, her tomboy sister, Arya.

Though it may appear at first that Sansa Stark is in love with the young prince Joffrey, what she is actually in love with is the central myth of her culture—that the king is kind and wise, that princes are noble and good, that ladies must be beautiful and behave in a ladylike manner. She continues to believe these myths even as events unfold that put the lie to them.

One of the first incidents that reveal the cracks in the façade of Sansa's world occurs when Joffrey, heir to the throne and

Sansa's betrothed, assaults a peasant boy, Mycah, who had been engaged in a mock duel with Arya Stark. During the course of this encounter, it becomes clear to the reader, if not to Sansa, that Joffrey is a bully and a coward, not the model of princely perfection starry-eyed Sansa assumes him to be. Joffrey tries to goad Mycah into fighting with him, and Arya steps in to protect her friend, who then runs off; as a peasant, Mycah knows that any encounter with nobility can result in death. Enraged, Joffrey turns on Arya, at which point Arya's pet direwolf, Nymeria, protects her.

Despite seeing Joffrey behave horribly toward a person of lesser status and try to hurt her own sister, Sansa clings to her belief that he's kind and good. So invested is she in her worldview that she does not question her beliefs even after she bears the brunt of Joffrey's anger herself. Later, when questioned by King Robert, Sansa lies and claims not to remember what happened. Sansa has been completely co-opted by Westeros's patriarchal culture, and it is only later, with her father's unjust execution and the ripping away of all her royal privileges, that she begins to see the truth behind the myth.

In the meantime, though, she is completely supportive of the culture and power structure of Westeros, the workings of which are on full display during the incident with Mycah. The children involved are between nine and thirteen years old, and yet they are already perfectly aware of the draconian rules of this society. When Arya defends Mycah against Joffrey, she steps outside the bounds of acceptable behavior (as she will for most of the series), and in doing so, takes a piece of traditionally male power for herself. This act is in and of itself transgressive, and both

Arya and Mycah know they are in profound physical danger, though Mycah realizes this before Arya does. When Arya finally comprehends the danger she and Nymeria are in, she drives the direwolf off to keep her from being killed. In a bit of stunning injustice, Sansa's wolf, Lady, is killed in Nymeria's place. In a way, the loss of the wolf represents a loss of connection to, and protection from, House Stark, whose symbol is the direwolf.

More importantly, the mock duel incident and its aftermath not only foreshadow events that will occur in King's Landing but also serve as examples of how those in positions of authority wield almost absolute power over everyone in Westeros. (And though the men are also constrained by this system, they have far more agency than the women and indeed exercise near-total control over the women around them.) A simple argument between children turns into a political incident, and terrible punishments are meted out the same for the young as they are for the adults—with no allowances made for their age.

Many readers find Sansa's travails during book one and the rest of the series to be extreme. She spends a great deal of time as a captive in Cersei's and Joffrey's court after her father is murdered. During this period she learns the true nature of the Lannisters and how precarious her own place is in the world, with her father dead and branded a traitor. Thereafter, she falls under the dubious protections of several men and is used as a pawn in other people's machinations. She survives all this by using the only tools she's developed within Westerosi culture: being submissive and hiding her true feelings.

To a large extent, Sansa's inability to recognize the gap between myth and reality cripples her. She truly believes in

the rules she has been taught about her society and her place
in it. And why shouldn't she embrace the culture of Westeros?
She's the eldest daughter of a powerful family. She's been raised
knowing she will one day wed into another powerful family.
In fact, once she is engaged to Joffrey, she has every reason to
believe she will be queen. And the world around her constantly
reinforces the notion that her own "virtues" have given rise to
her privileged situation. Yet those same traits make her incapable of functioning effectively, once those dreams are crushed
and reality intrudes.

Sansa is ill equipped for the chaotic time in which she finds
herself. She's passive, fearful, and often blinds herself to the
reality before her. Of the women discussed here, she's the only
one who fails to stand up for herself and take what personal
power she can. Eventually, she even appears to lose control of
her own identity, when she is cast as Alayne Stone, Lord Baelish's
illegitimate daughter. He tells her this is intended to protect her,
but he has other plans, intending to use her to make a claim
on Winterfell. To her credit, Sansa, who up until this point has
been surprised by the plots going on around her, appears to
grasp what Baelish is up to. Being exposed to the continual corruption around her, Sansa is slowly learning to trust no one and
to divine the power play in their every action.

These small, seemingly positive steps cannot fully convince
the reader that Sansa is free of her illusions, however. In fact,
it is because of her passivity that Sansa assumes these different
roles so easily. She dreamily floats along, allowing Baelish to set
a course for her life; she never takes the initiative. In situations
where she might begin to gain some personal power by refusing

to participate in Littlefinger's plans—or, like her sister Arya, concocting plans of her own—Sansa remains the passive pawn.

In this, she fills the role of the traditional princess of medieval fantasy. But in assigning her that role, Martin is making a powerful point about the dangers inherent in fantasy: how fanciful myths hide—and perpetuate—a fundamentally oppressive social structure. At every turn, Sansa's reality is unmoored. She experiences no pure and completely selfless knights, because they do not really exist. Her prince turns out to be a bully and a sociopath. After her father's death, every man who tries to help her is either weak or intent on using her for his own ends. And inasmuch as she cannot accept the world as it is, and not as the comforting stories have told her it should be, she remains powerless.

Arya Stark: The Rebel

If Sansa is the Good Girl, then Arya is in many ways her polar opposite: the Rebel. Arya is bored by all things considered "womanly." She doesn't give a fig for sewing, music, or being pretty; she'd rather shoot arrows, learn how to fight with a sword, and play-fight with the peasant boy Mycah.

Thanks to Arya's rebellious streak, she has the tools to survive after her father is murdered. But Arya's survival comes at a terrible price. She's stripped of her emotional innocence. Rage and bitterness at what has been done to her and her family will consume Arya throughout the books.

Like Sansa, Arya changes her identity over the course of the series. While their father was alive, Sansa and Arya were Starks,

Westerosi royalty. Once Ned is killed, their identities become murky. Because they are female, their identities are largely dependent on designations of male power—the rank, land holdings, and wealth of their fathers or husbands. Take those away and they become, in essence, no one, non-people. Disguises are a necessity for a young woman constantly in danger of being imprisoned, raped, or killed—particularly one who is of use as a political pawn. But a disguise can also be a tool with which a character can remake herself.

At first, it seems that Arya's disguises—her new identities—are molded by others. She is never as passive as Sansa; she proves herself quite capable of defending herself with Needle or just her fists. Yet Yoren shaves her head and dubs her Arry, and for a time she follows his lead—a choice that places her in peril. Even so, her willingness to throw off her gender demonstrates her understanding of the workings of power in her world. She can do things as a boy that would be denied her as a girl. And by the end of *A Clash of Kings* she has begun to fully take control of her identity and her fate, first by tricking Jaqen into helping her stage an uprising at Harrenhal to rescue the Northmen who had fought for her brother Robb, and then by recasting herself as Nymeria and fighting her way to freedom.

Arya is one of the most resilient characters in A Song of Ice and Fire. She survives through her wits, courage, and, perhaps more troubling, her rage. Unlike Sansa, who floats passively through the perils of her life, Arya insists on taking control. In a series where most of the likable characters die or are transformed in terrible ways, Arya grants the reader a slim hope for justice—even if it is of a rough variety.

Yet Arya's story is also a cautionary tale. Like all of the characters in A Song of Ice and Fire, Arya finds herself challenged and scarred by power. Though she proves masterful in exploiting power when given the opportunity, the emotional toll that fighting for every scrap of power takes on her is quite high. By the time she's ten, she's become inured to murder. When she ends up in Braavos in the House of Black and White, she is required to sacrifice all remaining vestiges of Arya Stark in order to gain abilities that will help her get revenge. She gives up her name, her family, and her possessions, only cheating a bit to keep her beloved sword, Needle—though that act apparently costs Arya her sight at the end of A Feast for Crows.

Her story provides a cautionary tale, yet the portrayal of Arya is predominantly positive. Arya bends but does not break, and illustrates the notion that those denied power can, out of necessity, develop ways to survive.

Brienne Tarth: The Outlier

If Arya and Sansa are the polar opposites, then Brienne is something altogether different and more rare in Westeros. She is a woman who moves through the world, having taken for herself most of the attributes of male power.

Brienne wears armor, carries a sword, is better at combat than most men, and wants nothing less than to be a knight— though, like Sansa, her notion of what being a knight means is based on a romanticized view of chivalry. Also like Sansa, she holds on to her romantic notions in the face of endless contradictory evidence.

Brienne suffers much abuse in the books at the hands of "courtly" knights. In *A Feast for Crows*, Brienne opens up to the Elder Brother while on her quest to find Sansa Stark. It's a poignant scene where she lays bare the difficulties of her life:

> "I am the only child the gods let him keep. The freakish one, one not fit to be son *or* daughter." All of it came pouring out of Brienne then, like black blood from a wound; the betrayals and betrothals, Red Ronnet and his rose, Lord Renly dancing with her, the wager for her maidenhead, the bitter tears she shed the night her king wed Margaery Tyrell, the mêlée at Bitterbridge, the rainbow cloak that she had been so proud of, the shadow in the king's pavilion, Renly dying in her arms, Riverrun and Lady Catelyn, the voyage down the Trident, dueling Jaime in the woods.

All of these parts of Brienne's life show the burden she endures for defying cultural expectations. How dare she not be born beautiful, failing to conform to what a woman "should" look like? How dare she wear male armor rather than attire more befitting a woman? And how dare she display her abilities as a fighter, abilities that are most certainly *not* in line with the Westerosi feminine ideal?

Brienne refuses to conform, even though she desires some of the things that would result from being a more compliant woman. She's a romantic, not unlike Sansa, though her expectations of being rewarded by her society are much lower than Sansa's as a result of her unconventional behavior. She seeks romance and is deeply in love with Renly Baratheon, one of the five kings with a claim to the Iron Throne. So great is her love for him that she offers the only thing she has that he might value: her life. She joins with him for his march on King's Landing and is later made part of his Rainbow Guard. Despite proving herself at Bitterbridge, she is viewed with contempt in Renly's camp and is made the butt of jokes about her appearance, as well as the object of crude jests about which knight will take her virginity.

The assumption by her fellow warriors that Brienne's sexuality is something to be coerced or taken, not something over which she has control, is telling of the wider perception of women in Westeros. So, too, the consistent rejection Brienne endures for failing to offer the men around her a pleasing countenance. No matter her skill as a knight, she is reminded time and again that a woman's primary function is to present herself in a manner appealing to men.

When Renly is murdered, Brienne is accused of the crime. She and Lady Catelyn flee together and eventually Brienne pledges loyalty to Catelyn, taking up the task of exchanging Jaime Lannister for Arya and Sansa Stark. Her devotion to this task remains unswerving, no matter the personal cost. In that, she remains a shining example of honor and dedication in a world where those things are more spoken of than practiced.

Because her actions fall consistently and fully outside the social norms, Brienne provides a stark lesson on how women who dare to take male power for their own are judged and treated not only in Westeros but in all conventionally patriarchal societies. She also remains a study in heartbreaking contradictions. She embraces the romantic ideals of her culture, both emotionally and through her actions, but is continually betrayed by the real world, simply because she cannot turn herself into the woman the Westerosi legends tell her she should be.

Cersei Lannister: The Evil Queen

There's no doubt that Cersei Lannister is one of the most appalling, wicked, and morally bankrupt characters in A Song of Ice and Fire—and that's saying a lot. While she conforms to most of the external conventions of womanhood in Westeros—she's pretty, has good manners, and is obedient . . . or appears to be— by the time the series opens, she has had her fill of her male-controlled universe.

In *A Game of Thrones*, Cersei commits a series of dark deeds. In a sadistic act of petty revenge, she has Sansa's direwolf, Lady, killed. She murders her husband, setting in motion many of the horrors that ensue. She has Ned Stark imprisoned and branded as a traitor. She sets her sociopathic son, Joffrey—who is a result of her affair with her brother, Jaime—on the throne, hoping to rule Westeros through him. All the while, she's manipulating everyone she can to achieve her own ends.

Cersei is a mass of female rage, much of it justified. Her arranged marriage, a pairing that she actually wanted (making her one of the luckier women in Westeros), was spoiled on her wedding night when Robert came to their marriage bed drunk and with the name of another woman on his lips. She never forgets this slight, and her marriage becomes a vehicle for humiliating Robert in every way possible. Like Sansa, she is privileged and enjoys all the benefits this implies, but wounded by Robert's many betrayals, she throws off the societal rules that constrain her behavior.

Cersei strives to gain power any way she can. She sleeps with her twin brother and passes their children off as the heirs to the throne. In Westeros, as with many male-dominated societies, a man's power lies not just in himself but also in the line of sons he leaves behind. Cersei usurps the line of succession, substituting another man's child for Robert's own, an act that is both treason and the ultimate emasculation. The only sons who will sit on the Iron Throne after Robert dies are those of the queen's Lannister bloodline alone. That they are children by her twin implies a mirroring of herself in their creation, a startling statement of control and self-defined identity.

Cersei takes action to address her frustrations in ways that are abhorrent. However, nothing she does is terribly different from the behavior of any of the kings who've sat on the Iron Throne. For example, one of Robert Baratheon's most noteworthy decisions in the series is to send an assassin to kill Daenerys Targaryen. Murder as a tool of politics is fair game for queens as well as kings. The Targaryen kings routinely married their siblings, making Cersei's incest less aberrant than it might appear. The history of the Iron Throne is one of brutality, murder, and manipulation, and Cersei is merely utilizing the standard toolset to achieve her aspirations of power.

Like Arya and Brienne, Cersei wields power by adopting the strategies and behaviors of the patriarchy more often than the ones more routinely available to women. It's telling that she's judged negatively while the men who use similar tactics are celebrated as legends. In this, she reveals the hypocrisy at the heart of Westerosi culture just as surely as poor, deluded Sansa.

Daenerys Targaryen: The New Woman

Daenerys Targaryen is the most powerful woman in the known world. She is introduced in *A Game of Thrones* as a terrorized, weak-willed little girl who wants nothing more than to appease her violent brother and help him win back the Iron Throne. (In choosing appeasement she isn't so very different from Sansa, though her path through life ends up being very different.) By the end of the book, she has immolated herself on her husband's pyre and magically risen from the ashes in possession of three baby dragons. There haven't been dragons in Westeros for hundreds of years, and as she awakens the dragons, she also awakens in herself a mystical knowledge that *she*—not her brother, Viserys—may be the true inheritor of the Iron Throne.

Daenerys's journey from child bride to first female ruler of a *khalasar* is one of the more dramatic examples in the Ice and Fire series of a woman taking power. However, hers is not a journey without problems—both for the character and for readers. The most obvious of these is the fact that she falls in love with Khal Drogo. For a modern reader, this is inevitably problematic—being a mere thirteen, she can hardly be said to have consented to her marriage, much less to the sexual acts that take place within it. However, in Westerosi society, she's considered of marriageable age once she has physically matured to a point where she can bear children. Her emotional maturity and personal desire for the union are irrelevant in a culture where the woman's role is to bear a man's children and to submit to him.

Daenerys is sold to Khal Drogo by her brother, whose goal is to use the khal's men to invade Westeros and regain the throne he believes is his birthright. And Daenerys understands that being bartered off to a powerful savage, to cement a political and military alliance, is simply part of the role women must play in her culture.

It's clear that Viserys has been emotionally abusing Daenerys for years. It's also clear that she has internalized this abuse, as she often makes excuses for his behavior. She accepts her situation *vis-à-vis* her brother, her status, and her forced marriage, even as she fears the outcome. Like Sansa Stark, Daenerys doesn't question the world in which she lives.

Because she has been bartered like chattel, coerced into a marriage about which she has no say, Daenerys's first sexual experience is, unsurprisingly and disturbingly, as a victim of rape at the hands of her new husband. Though she "willingly" goes with Khal Drogo, she cannot be said to have consented. She doesn't want to have sex with him. Her agreement to the sex act takes place under duress. And, as she has no true agency of her own, she cannot truly agree to her role in the bargain Viserys has made.

By modern standards, if not those of Westeros, age and coercion make every sexual encounter Daenerys has with Khal Drogo amount to ongoing marital rape. Eventually, she does take control of their sexual life, after learning ways to manipulate Drogo sexually. It could be argued that this was her way of regaining power. However, the canard of the woman who falls in love with her rapist is extremely difficult to overcome for many readers.

And it may be that we aren't meant to overcome it.

There's an enormous amount of violence against women in A Song of Ice and Fire, and its portrayal is uniformly negative. It is always uncomfortable rather than titillating. Rape and sexual violence, both from "protectors" and from strangers, are persistent threats to all the female characters. Robert Baratheon drunkenly rapes Cersei; when she tells him he's hurt her, he blames it on alcohol. Sansa, Arya, and Brienne all experience verbal threats of sexual violence from a wide variety of men. This omnipresent threat in these women's lives creates what amounts to an environment of sexual oppression. That this circumstance is rarely remarked upon by the characters shows just how entrenched it is in the culture.

Given her circumstance, Daenerys has only two real options. She can either resist Khal Drogo—a losing proposition both for her and for Viserys—or she can find a way to live with her situation. She chooses the latter. With this choice, she begins to gain power, first through Khal Drogo, who grants her both his protection and the authority that comes from being his mate, and, later, through her own agency when she emerges unscathed from Khal Drogo's funeral pyre with the baby dragons. Only with Khal Drogo's death is she free to make her way in the world, largely unencumbered by male control.

Of course, none of this power comes without a price. As she gathers her army together, Daenerys begins to sacrifice aspects of her personality. She becomes harder and less compassionate, her choices less personal. A sweetness that she had at the beginning of the series is slowly burning away as she becomes more and more powerful.

The Price to Be Paid

These female characters, along with many others in the series, are a striking group of powerful women making their way through a patriarchal world where the mere fact of their gender would deny them power.

Sansa, Arya, Cersei, Brienne, and Daenerys are all on journeys to create a place in the world for themselves in the face of massive obstacles thrown at them by an oppressive society. Though their paths through this maze toward autonomy are different, most of them seek the same thing: control over their own lives.

Sansa loses her power within the culture after her father is killed. She lives her life buffeted by others, refusing to take any action that would create a more autonomous life for herself. Arya seeks to avenge those who have wronged her by seizing power where and when she can—no matter that the kinds of power available to her drive her further and further from the girl she once was. Cersei takes power through guile, manipulation, and murder. She's indifferent to how the power affects her because power is the only thing she understands and values. Brienne adopts the trappings of masculine power even though it makes her a pariah and the butt of jokes. Her power is blunted both by her own self-loathing and the approbation of the culture around her. Daenerys is the one woman who holds her life in her own hands. Orphaned, widowed, possessing real power—in the form of the dragons, her own possibly magical nature, and the warriors at her command—there are no men who rule her.

Unfortunately, power comes at a cost to all these women, just as it does to the men who wield it. Such is the nature of power in A Song of Ice and Fire.

In Westeros, George R.R. Martin has created a brutal world where unspeakable acts are commonplace, where the shares of power allotted to men and women are clearly out of balance, where women must struggle, steal, and fight for every ounce of autonomy. The stories of Arya, Cersei, and all the other female characters are harsh, but they shine an even harsher light on their society and the lies that poison its heart. And that's where Martin does something remarkable. In the midst of what appears to be a traditional male-power fantasy about war and politics, he serves up a grim, realistic, and harrowing depiction of what happens when women aren't fully empowered in a society. In doing so, by creating such diverse and fully rendered female characters and thrusting them into this grim and bitter world, Martin has created a subversively feminist tale.

◆ ◆ ◆

CAROLINE SPECTOR has been an editor and writer in the science fiction, fantasy, and gaming fields for the last twenty-five years. Most recently, she has had stories in the Wild Cards collections *Inside Straight*, *Busted Flush*, and *Suicide Kings*. Before joining the Wild Cards consortium, Caroline authored three novels—*Scars*, *Little Treasures*, and *Worlds Without End*—editions of which have been published in English, French, German, and Hungarian. She has written and edited several adventure modules and sourcebooks for TSR's game lines, most notably *Top Secret/S.I.* and *Marvel Super Heroes Roleplaying*, both on her own and co-authored with her husband, gaming legend Warren Spector. In addition to her writing, Caroline spent two years as Associate Editor at the magazine *Amazing Stories*.

◆ JOHN JOS. MILLER ◆

COLLECTING ICE AND FIRE IN THE AGE OF NOOK AND KINDLE

GEORGE R.R. MARTIN'S EPIC fantasy A Song of Ice and Fire, currently incomplete at five volumes, is a book world rarity: a genre series that has broken through the walls of the fantasy/science fiction ghetto. It's immensely popular among mainstream readers and critics and is garnering a lot of attention in academic circles, even before the final book in the series has been published.

Although concrete, reliable data is hard to come by, it seems fair to say that Ice and Fire has sold at least 15 million copies worldwide, though this is without sales from the most recently published volume, *A Dance with Dragons*. It has been widely reported that *Dance* sold more copies on its first day of availability than any other book in 2012, totaling 298,000 copies (170,000

in hardback; 110,000 as an e-book; and 18,000 as an audiobook).
Total sales to date are unknown, or at least so far unpublished.

There are several good reasons for its astounding popularity.
The world of Ice and Fire is epic in scope, peopled by dozens
of carefully delineated characters, and written in wonderfully
descriptive prose. A masterfully produced, written, and acted
television adaptation of Martin's universe doesn't hurt, either,
drawing in a multitude of readers who would otherwise have
not been aware of the novels.

A Song of Ice and Fire also sits directly astride the e-book/paper
book publishing chasm. Although this doesn't entirely account
for its widespread popularity, I suspect that embracing the new
publishing technology has something to do with its phenomenal
success. *A Game of Thrones*, the first volume in the series, was
published in 1996 before there were such things as e-books. The
most recent volume, *A Dance with Dragons*, appeared in 2011,
a time of booming e-book sales. What does this mean for readers in general and, more germane to this article, book collectors
specifically? Obviously, the final words in this debate are yet to be
spoken, but we can make some educated guesses.

The first of Martin's Ice and Fire volumes to have a simultaneous e-book/paper copy release was *A Feast for Crows* in
2005. Around that time earlier volumes were also translated to
the e-book format. *A Dance with Dragons* had a simultaneous
e-book/paper copy release, as presumably will later volumes in
the series. For the first few titles e-book sales lagged behind even
audiobooks, but with the publication of *Dance* sales for e-book
and hardcover releases are, according to Martin, running neck
and neck. Sales patterns are clearly shifting and will likely tilt

further in the future. To what ultimate end is currently uncertain, though I doubt that the proliferation of e-books means the end of paper editions.

Several factors contribute to this belief. First, collectible book sales remain unaffected by the advent of e-publishing. More detail is presented below, but publishers, both large and small, continue to eagerly produce various Ice and Fire editions, and once purchased, their owners are quite reluctant to part with them.

Humanity can be sorted into—among other things— collectors and noncollectors. To be up front about my own bias, I'm firmly in the collectors' camp. I enjoy the process of finding and acquiring objects (including books) that interest me, and I enjoy owning things that have an actual physical existence. To me and many others, collecting is a primal urge equivalent to eating and sleeping. This trait is not going to disappear from human nature anytime soon.

Some changes in the publishing world are coming, though. The rising popularity of e-books probably means the death of the mass market paperback. This is not necessarily a bad thing, as return policies associated with this format—specifically, cover stripping for return and the shredding of the book's body—are both costly and wasteful. E-readers are a convenient, easy, and increasingly affordable alternative to shipping masses of books that ultimately go unsold and are eventually pulped for little purpose.

Also, many limited editions are produced by small publishers, not the huge ones owned by multinational corporations. (There are exceptions; as an example, see the HarperCollins slipcased editions of the Ice and Fire books.) These small publishers largely have a better sense of aesthetics than the utterly profit-driven multinationals. But even the giants can and do produce superlative volumes when the mood strikes, as with the signed and limited editions of the Robert Silverberg–edited *Legends*.

Although today's economic climate is tough, there are a multitude of small and not-so-small presses producing short-run first editions of highly artistic limited editions, not only of Martin's work, but of a wide range of authors in the science fiction and fantasy field. In fact, there are probably so many limited editions that only the most well-heeled collectors can even attempt a complete genre collection, which was something that could be fairly easily done in earlier decades.

Despite hand-wringing from the doomsayers—which has been going on since well before Dickens; I suspect that if there'd been publishers in Homer's time, he'd have heard pretty much the same poor-mouthing as we do today—the publishing industry is not going to go away anytime soon. Both e-books and paper books will remain part of their business model, in some proportion or another, for the foreseeable future. That's not to say that ideas of what constitute a book or even publication are not changing.

Since the proliferation of e-books makes revision easy for even published texts, an artistic question arises regarding the concept of the "finished work." Some authors—particular examples in the science fiction and fantasy field are Michael Moorcock and F. Paul Wilson—frequently revisit older works, polishing or even substantially altering them to fit more readily into a series framework.

As a reader and collector both, I have mixed feelings about this practice, but it seems Ice and Fire fans have little to worry about on this score. Martin has no plans to revise earlier volumes. "The work is the work," he told me not long ago. "Nothing has been cut from it, so there's nothing to put back in." Any side-trips into his universe will continue with shorter works (e.g., the Dunk and Egg stories) to illuminate incidents outside the main story. There will be no need to collect later editions of Ice and Fire volumes to remain *au courant* with the finished story.

If you are going to collect any editions of the series, there are some things you should probably consider.

As with any field of collectibles, book collectors have constructed their own set of rules, a shared common wisdom, built up over centuries of experience, though personally I regard these rules, as the saying goes, more as guidelines. Shape your collection the way you want, not by strict laws that might diminish your enjoyment. For example, common wisdom says that if you collect signed books you should have the author write just his or her name—called "flatsigning"—without a personal inscription, because some dealers believe that a flatsigned book is easier to sell and thus more valuable than one signed, "To My Dearest Humperdink."

I think that's a mistake. First, I don't particularly care how much my collection will someday sell for, because when it's dispersed I'll be dead and its monetary value will be entirely irrelevant to me. Second, I enjoy signed books because of the sense of personal connection they gives you to the authors. An inscribed book entails a closer connection than one simply signed. Even if the book isn't inscribed to me personally, the sentiment reveals something of the author's thoughts and personality. To me that makes the volume more interesting and thus more valuable than a simple signature.

But that's me. As a collector you should follow your own rules. With that in mind, though, there are some basic parameters that lift an ordinary volume into the collectible class. These parameters fall into three areas: primacy, scarcity, and aesthetics. Once these factors are taken into consideration, condition also comes into play. I shall briefly examine these categories as they pertain to collectibility, then relate them to the Ice and Fire books.

Primacy relates to the notion of first edition, which may be more complicated than you think. Collectors value the earliest iteration of a title. Information regarding this can usually be found on the indicia or copyright page, which appears after the title page and before the text begins. Although for some publishers in certain time periods this information is tricky to interpret, it's completely straightforward for all the Ice and Fire books. I'll use just one as an example, but the data is presented in a similar manner for all. The American first edition of the first volume, *A Game of Thrones*, reads:

A Bantam/Spectra Book / September 1996
10 9 8 7 6 5 4 3 2 1

The first British edition reads:

HarperCollins Publisher 1996/123456789

The numbers refer to the specific print run (more on which can be found below).

Sometimes fine distinctions are made when changes occur partway through a print run, such as a change in color or minor textual addition or subtraction on the dust jacket. Varieties such as these are called "states," and again, it's up to the individual collector to decide what's significant enough to him or her to worry about. Fortunately, this complication doesn't apply to Ice and Fire because no distinctions of state have arisen, at least in the British and American editions.

The notion of "first edition" is also blurred by some sellers who describe a particular book as "first edition, nth printing." The number of a specific book's actual print run can be found among the indicia, as noted above. I've frequently observed this distinction in listings of Ice and Fire titles. Again, it's up to individual collectors, but for the most part you will not find much of a premium on early, but non-first, print runs for any of the Ice and Fire books.

Scarcity is somewhat related to primacy. First editions commonly have smaller print runs than accumulated later editions, and the initial book in a successful series usually has a smaller first print run than subsequent titles. That's certainly the case with Ice and Fire. The series has grown enormously more popular with each volume, so each subsequent title has larger and larger first editions. Only a few thousand copies were printed in the original edition of *A Game of Thrones* compared to several hundred thousand for *A Dance with Dragons*. All five books have gone through numerous printings and editions. Although trade paperbacks and mass market paperbacks of *Dance* haven't appeared as of this writing, it's only a matter of time until they do.

Once Ice and Fire had become well established, Meisha Merlin published a limited, signed edition with extensive artwork by notable science fiction and fantasy artists. These books instantly became a big hit on the collectible book market. When Merlin went out of business, Subterranean Press took over the limited edition niche with *A Storm of Swords* and will undoubtedly continue through to the end of the series. They have also announced plans to republish the two Meisha Merlin volumes in a format identical to the Subterranean volumes. This is an unusual circumstance, but it shows the continually increasing popularity of the series. My guess is that these volumes will also be eagerly embraced by the collector community.

Limited editions are highly sought after because of the (usual) high aesthetic quality of their design, which include such elements as special slipcases, fine endpapers, page edge gilding, and reams of artwork by the finest artists in the field. Throw in autographs by author and artists with guaranteed authentic signatures, and print runs limited to the hundreds rather than the thousands produced by the big publishers, and you have a product popular among discerning collectors of the particular writer, the genre, or even simply fine art and writing in general.

Meisha Merlin published 448 numbered copies and 52 lettered (a to zz) copies of *A Game of Thrones* in 2002 and *A Clash of Kings* in 2005. These volumes sold well even before publication, since collectors routinely preorder or subscribe to the entire series. Generally speaking, similarly numbered or lettered sets are preferable to sets with varied numbers or letters but, of course, are also much harder to assemble if you're late to the game.

Subterranean Press, taking up the Ice and Fire gauntlet when Merlin went out of business, produced similar quantities of numbered and lettered editions of *A Storm of Swords* in 2008 and *A Feast for Crows* in 2009, with plans to continue the series as more titles become available. *A Dance with Dragons* is scheduled for publication in the spring of 2012. As previously mentioned, they also have plans to release their own versions of the first two titles. Their format is different than Merlin's, with each title broken into two volumes.

It would be difficult to form a collection of the limiteds at this late date. Current owners of these volumes are proving quite loyal to the series and are either unwilling to sell their copies or, if willing, believe almost universally that the market will go nowhere but up.

The following information, taken from the AbeBooks website, which has 40,000,000 books for sale in its database, is a snapshot of the market in a precise moment of time (in this case, early December 2011) but adequately reflects the general state of availability and cost of the Ice and Fire titles.

The only Meisha Merlin/Subterranean Press limited editions currently on the market are a complete set of the first four titles. The set is from the numbered release (#38) and is described as "as new." The asking price is $10,000.

If collecting the early limited editions seems impossible at this time, there is always the first editions to fall back on. Ice and Fire has had remarkable success throughout the world, so you may be interested in acquiring the first edition in your native language, but the very popularity of the series, which has appeared in dozens of countries in almost every major language around the world, makes it impossible to examine non-English editions in any detail.

Instead, I will establish publication primacy in the English language. Fortunately, with one somewhat tricky exception, that's easy. I first laid out the groundwork for identifying the first worldwide editions in an article for *Firsts* magazine, "Collecting George R.R. Martin," back in 2001.

A Game of Thrones is the tricky one. Supposedly released simultaneously by HarperCollins Voyager (UK) and Bantam Spectra (US) in 1996, the Bantam American release is the true first wordwide edition, actually preceding the British edition into print by several months. Although the indicia page of the Bantam edition lists the publication date as September, Bantam actually rushed *Game* into print for the American Booksellers Association convention in May 1996. Additional copies also were distributed at the Westercon science fiction convention over the 1996 Fourth of July weekend.

This is good news for collectors who collect worldwide firsts. Although the initial print run for Bantam's *A Game of Thrones* was rather small, it certainly eclipsed HarperCollins' UK run of 1,500 copies, especially considering that many of the HarperCollins books were purchased by libraries and are precluded from the collectors' market by condition problems.

The HarperCollins editions of the next three titles, *A Clash of Kings* (1998), *A Storm of Swords* (2000), and *A Feast for Crows* (2005), were all released prior to the Bantam US editions and are the worldwide firsts.

A Dance with Dragons was a simultaneous 2011 release in America and the United Kingdom by their respective publishers, so basically they could be described as co-firsts. However, Martin has brought up an interesting point. Both British and American bookstores held midnight release parties on the first "day" of the book's official release. And it must be admitted that midnight falls first in Britain. Is that enough to establish primacy for the British edition? I'll leave that to the individual collector to ponder.

Primacy is thus established for the Bantam (American) edition for the first volume, the HarperCollins (British) editions for the next three, with the fifth having co-firsts. Given the essential impossibility of collecting the British editions, many collectors, especially Americans, have been content to target the Bantam editions as firsts. Of course, they are obviously the American firsts.

Other printings and editions for all titles, with different covers and in different formats, quickly followed. Some—for example, the HarperCollins slipcased hardcovers, limited to a thousand sets—may ultimately prove popular with collectors. The only limited editions considered here, however, are the Meisha Merlin/Subterranean Press numbered/lettered editions, due to their scarcity, artistic quality, and publisher-authenticated signatures of artists and authors.

Once factors of primacy remove later printings and editions from collectible consideration, condition becomes important. There's no science to ascertaining condition, despite what the coin, baseball card, and comic book graders would have you believe. It's all opinion. Granted, experienced, educated opinion is worth more than naive, hopeful, or (especially) unscrupulous opinion. If you enter any field of collecting, you must educate yourself on its standards and gain a knowledgeable opinion about any object you plan to acquire.

The number of Ice and Fire books in the various first print runs, especially for the first three volumes, are limited, but we must also remember that all were recently published. As such, only those books in top condition, Near Fine or better—dust jacket and book itself—can be considered collectible.

There's no doubt that the American Bantam editions are more common than the HarperCollins UK editions, though common in this case is a relative term. The only HarperCollins firsts for sale on AbeBooks are copies of *A Dance with Dragons*. I knew that *A Game of Thrones* was a scarce title, but I was surprised to find the first four books totally absent. Even *A Dance with Dragons* was scarce, with only six copies in collectible condition listed. Prices ranged from $153 to $65, with an average of $103. Note that all of these copies are signed, which adds a premium to their value. Note also that Martin is a willing and frequent signer and many signed copies of his books can be found on the market.

Many dealers are advertising the HarperCollins slipcased hardcovers as first editions, with asking prices for signed copies of *A Game of Thrones* as high as $350 and as low as about $50. By no means should these later editions be considered firsts. It remains to be seen what impact they will make on the collectors' market.

The Bantam editions are somewhat more common. Let's start with complete sets, for those who are really late to the game. If you'd like to acquire all the Bantam firsts in one swoop, a set of all five in Near Fine or better is available for $3,000.

All the copies enumerated below are in collectible condition (Near Fine or better), book and dust jacket both.

A Game of Thrones shows eight copies available, all signed, ranging in price from $1,500 to $500, with an average price of $956. When I did the *Firsts* article in 2001, the price range for this title was $250 to $300.

A Clash of Kings shows two signed copies available at $650 and $575; average $612. Three unsigned copies were also available with prices ranging from $250 to $150, averaging $200. In 2001 the price range for this volume was $30 to $50.

A Storm of Swords is represented by four signed copies at $300 to $140; average $216. One unsigned copy was listed at $115. In 2001, this title was selling for $15 to $30.

A Feast for Crows has five signed titles at $300 to $50; average $153. There was one unsigned copy at $60.

A Dance with Dragons, with by far the largest first print run, has a relatively small population of twenty-four signed copies at $150 to $49 (average $82) and four unsigned at $40 to $31 (average $35). I would have thought there'd be more copies available. I would suggest checking used bookstores, but remember, again, you're looking for first printings. Even though there were several hundred thousand, many seem to have already disappeared into the hands of the general reading public, who on the whole don't know or care about the difference between a first edition or a book club edition. That can be good news for a determined (and lucky) collector.

The existence of e-book editions for all titles has had no discernible effect on the collectors' market. Some time, obviously, the market will peak and prices will stabilize, but I don't think we'll see this for a while.

It might not be a bad idea to snatch up those available unsigned firsts of *A Dance with Dragons* and hope that George will appear in your area soon.

◆ ◆ ◆

JOHN JOS. MILLER has had about ten novels and twice as many short stories published, as well as comic book scripts, gaming books for the Wild Cards series, and over a hundred posts for the blog cheesemagnet.com. He also has written extensively on baseball history, especially nineteenth-century baseball and the Negro Leagues. He is one of the original members of the New Mexican group that created the superheroes-in-prose franchise Wild Cards. Besides having stories in three of the titles currently available from Tor Books, he has also authored two RPG volumes about Wild Cards for Green Ronin Publishing. His adaptation of George R.R. Martin's "In the House of the Worm," a Gothic horror story that takes place in the far future on a dying Earth, will be published by Avatar Press whenever the artist finally gets around to finishing it. His columns on cheesemagnet.com deal mainly with fantastic cinema and fiction. He also frequently gives away books and movies, so you should check it out just for the swag alone.

BEYOND THE GHETTO

How George R.R. Martin Fights the Genre Wars

WHAT'S THE HARDEST PART of writing a book? It's a good question—one I get often from aspiring authors wary of the pain—but the answer is never what people think. Beginning can be hard, yes, and ending can be downright brutal, as the protracted wait for *A Dance with Dragons* demonstrated, but the hardest part comes once you've finished your book and sold it. Then you must make a searching and fearless moral inventory and *try to get blurbs*. Securing other authors' positive comments on your work is the closest you will probably come to asking out your celebrity crush; my strategy is to beg.

When I set out to get blurbs for a young adult novel with fantasy elements that I sold in 2010, the person I wanted to beg most was George R.R. Martin. While reading up on roleplaying games' influence on American culture, I discovered his work through *Dreamsongs: Volume II,* which, if you're already chafing for *The Winds of Winter,* documents Martin's creative ventures in Los Angeles with Tyrion-esque cynicism. In *Dreamsongs* I found that in 1983 Martin started playing the *Call of Cthulhu* and *Superworld* games so much that he *stopped writing for a year and nearly went broke.* As he explained in an introduction to the Wild Cards novels that resulted from his obsession: "[My wife] Parris used to listen at my office door, hoping to hear the clicking of my keyboard from within, only to shudder at the ominous rattle of dice."

This was the first time I'd read about a writer having a fantasy gaming problem, as opposed to, say, a drug or alcohol problem. Since I'd recently weathered my own ten-year addiction to *Magic: The Gathering,* I saw a kindred spirit in Martin, someone who might understand me—and dig my book. My publisher approved of my blurb quest, as Martin is a phenomenal success, with more than 8.5 million books sold in the Song of Ice and Fire series according to *USA Today.* But those sales are supported by a surprising development for an author steeped in roleplaying games and genre fiction—canonical critical acclaim. *Time Magazine* gave Martin the ultimate blurb in 2005: "the American Tolkien."

But when did that become a distinction? Tolkien has been part of our culture for so long that it's easy to forget that The Lord of the Rings was derided as escapist—and worse, foreign—when it first appeared here. You can get a sense of just how harsh the criticisms were in Michael Saler's excellent 2012 critical overview of fantasy, *As If: Modern Enchantment and the*

Literary Prehistory of Virtual Reality, from Oxford University Press. "Certain people—especially, perhaps, in Britain—have a lifelong appetite for juvenile trash," declared Edmund Wilson in 1956. "What apparently gets kids square in their post-adolescent sensibilities is not the scholarly top-dressing but the undemanding, comfortable, child-sized story underneath," chided *Life.*

This argument—that fantasy is simple, formulaic, and for children—has kept it in a genre ghetto since its inception as a modern literary form in the nineteenth century. Although it has been creeping into academia for years, and Martin has accelerated its move toward acceptance by serious circles like the *New York Times Book Review*, it is still dismissed by many critics as by-the-numbers hackwork created to serve a market: nerds like me, Martin, and, let's face it, you. Fantasy's story, from formulation through critical dismissal to massive popular success and overdue academic assessment, is part of an ongoing intellectual conflict as grueling as the War of the Ninepenny Kings—*the genre wars*—that is only now approaching detente.

◆ ◆ ◆

More than anything, "genre" is a marketing term. It's meant to help booksellers shelve product, and thus it doesn't have much relevance prior to the ascendance of the book as a mass-market product in England in the mid-1800s, where reduced printing costs led to an explosion of garishly illustrated "penny dreadfuls." These serialized entertainments, marketed as literature to lower- and middle-class readers, forced critics to draw the first line in the genre wars: between "literary" and "popular" fiction.

It was clear to academics that the work of, say, George W.M. Reynolds (who never used the word "face" when "countenance" would suffice, and avoided "said" in favor of "ejaculated") was not literature. It had to be something else, and "crap" seemed impolite. The problem was, people *loved* it: in ten years, according to The Victorian Web, Reynolds moved over a million copies of *The Mysteries of London* and its sequel *The Mysteries of the Court of London*, which would make them bestsellers even today. "Popular" fiction seemed a safe place to sequester his output from serious work.

Yet even when separated from literature, popular fiction was seen as a threat. Henry James warned against it in his 1884 essay "The Art of Fiction," aiming squarely at Robert Louis Stevenson, who had just written the well-liked adventure tale *Treasure Island*. For James, "a novelist writes out of and about 'all experience' and aims to represent nothing less than 'life' itself in all its complexities," says Ken Gelder in his 2004 survey *Popular Fiction: The Logics and Practices of a Literary Field*. In contrast, "*Treasure Island* [. . .] is nothing more than a fantasy."

Stevenson responded in an essay of his own, "speaking up precisely for those qualities found in 'the novel of adventure' that Henry James had so disdained: a plot or a 'story', as well as 'danger', 'passion' and 'intrigue'." Hidden in this defense lies the problem that still hampers fantasy fiction today: "danger" and "intrigue" are one thing, and they're both in heroic supply in A Song of Ice and Fire, but what makes a bookseller shelve a novel under "fantasy" is often that it stars a farm boy who doesn't realize he's a prince; or a farm boy who has to face a series of challenges having to do with earth, fire, water, and air. The persistence of cliché in fantasy allows critics in the Jamesian tradition to continue to dismiss it as writing for children, whereas Stevenson and his contemporaries preferred to think of themselves as pioneers of the imagination.

◆ ◆ ◆

Imagination was a dangerous force in nineteenth-century Europe. Polite people were not supposed to imagine too much, lest they suffer like two causalities of earlier skirmishes in the genre wars: Madame Bovary, who read too many romance novels, or Don Quixote, who read too many knight's tales. Real literature was supposed to be set in the real world, where real-world people navigated real-world problems. As Rousseau argued in 1762: "The real world has its limits, the imaginary world is infinite. Unable to enlarge the one, let us restrict the other."

But imagination did have its place among the masses, in folklore, satire, and children's literature such as *Alice in Wonderland* (1865). In the guise of juvenile fiction, fantastical tales were acceptable even for upper-class readers, some of whom, like Stevenson, grew up to be authors who couldn't constrain themselves to the realist mode sanctioned by the Enlightenment. They produced books at the turn of the twentieth century that embraced impossibility but were grounded in reality. Jules Verne called them "*Les Voyages Extraordinaires*"; H.G. Wells called them "scientific romance," and that term works for me: it spells out the books' necessary characteristics of fantastic premises and empirical prose.

In part, scientific romance—which included *King Solomon's Mines* (1885) by H. Rider Haggard, *The Gods of Pegāna* (1905) by Lord Dunsany, and *With the Night Mail* (1909) by Rudyard Kipling—was a response to the antiseptic climate ushered in by the modern era. At the end of the nineteenth century, science was honing in on the most basic explanations of the natural world. (Or so we thought; nobody ever expected us to need CERN.) People had a chance to completely separate themselves from spiritual meaning—to abandon their souls in favor of cold, hard intellect—and the departure of magic from everyday life left a void. Scientific romance strove to fill that void while remaining true to the secularism that the modern world demanded. That meant presenting stories as if they were nonfiction, complete with glossaries, footnotes, and that essential component of today's fantasy novel: the map. By buffeting their imaginative texts with ancillary paratexts, these authors anticipated the contemporary fantasy writer's task of world-building, going behind the scenes to create a coherent world that readers could make their own.

◆   ◆   ◆

This new movement demanded critical attention. For one thing, scientific romance writers outstripped George W.M. Reynolds and the penny-dreadful crowd in sheer skill. Wells, Verne, and Kipling weren't hacks; they were gifted if workmanlike storytellers who exhibited a legitimate, cohesive response to the modern era. Their books also became beloved around the world, even by children who would later become intellectuals. As Jean-Paul

Sartre says of Verne: "When I opened [his books], I forgot about everything. Was that reading? No, but it was death by ecstasy." If you've lost weeks to A Song of Ice and Fire, you know what he's talking about.

Yet the success of scientific romance did not sway critics, who accused it of being juvenile, having undeveloped characters, and not engaging the problems of the real world. Luckily for them, they soon had a more specific ghetto to place it in: "science fiction & fantasy."

This dual category, since formally split by critic Darko Suvin but still found in many bookstores with that dragon-like ampersand, was established in America in the early twentieth century through the pulp magazines. Like genre itself, the pulps were a marketing construct created, according to Richard Mathews's *Fantasy: The Liberation of Imagination*, to compete with popular-fiction dime novels. Through them, several major forerunners of George R.R. Martin first saw print, and within their pages many clichés were established that still dog fantasy: swords and sorcery, swords and sandals, and evil, sexy sorceresses. H.P. Lovecraft, who used the format to create a world of alien gods, felt that traditional fantasy stories were useless, as does Tyrion Lannister in *A Dance with Dragons*: "Talking dragons, dragons hoarding gold and gems [. . .] nonsense, all of it." Lovecraft in particular went through great pains to create empirical backdrops for his tales, including the *Necronomicon*, an invented book of dark magic that has since been published in several versions. Unfortunately he had little success in his lifetime—and in death Edmund Wilson dismissed his oeuvre as "a boy's game."

Yet outside the realm of literary criticism, pulp readers were treating "science fiction & fantasy" as more than a game. They were discussing it extensively and building the groundwork for what we now call "fandom." Hugo Gernsback, editor of *Amazing Stories,* did the movement an immense service by publishing the addresses of those who sent in letters, enabling readers to contact one another directly to discuss the work. By the middle of the twentieth century, genre outsold literary fiction by something like nine to one . . . yet it continued to founder in the critical establishment, which had doubled down on its commitment to real-world settings. Serious literature was "defined by most critics as narrative realism and admitted nothing that was nonrealistic," according to Ken Keegan in 2006's *ParaSpheres: Extending Beyond the Spheres of Literary and Genre Fiction*; nowhere in the vast stylistic void between Joyce and Hemingway was there room for a dragon or a flying god.

With the position of the establishment essentially unchanged for a century, genre readers couldn't wait for academics to lend structure and insight to their obsessions. They formed a para-academic environment of bookshops, fanzines, and "Letters" pages in the pulps—and, later, comic books—to analyze the work in the context of its ever-lengthening history. One active participant in this culture was George R.R. Martin, whose fan letters mark his first appearances in print. In 1965's *Avengers* #12, he praises "the fast-paced action, solid characterization, and that terrific ending," some of the same characteristics Stevenson brought up in his defense of "the novel of adventure." Thus the champions of fantasy moved from responding to Henry James to writing letters to Stan Lee—even after the cultural supernova of The Lord of the Rings. Things weren't looking good for fantasy in the genre wars.

◆ ◆ ◆

Enter *A Game of Thrones*, published as a genre title in 1996 to suspected commercial super-success. With Robert Jordan's Wheel of Time saga a hot commodity, publishers entered a fierce bidding war for what was then conceived as the Song of Fire and Ice *trilogy*. Subsequent sales have overshadowed the fact that *Thrones* was not an immediate hit, but rather a slow burn, encouraged by independent booksellers, reviewers, and a Locus Award for Best Fantasy Novel. In retrospect it's easy to see why: Martin grew up in a world where fantasy's rules were well established, but he had the courage to break those rules in ways that challenged critics—and readers.

The continuum of genre writers from the scientific romance to today established tropes for fantasy that are less obvious and more insidious than the wizard in the black hat or the gruff dwarf. One, identified in John H. Timmerman's *Other Worlds: the Fantasy Genre* (1983), is "commonness of character." The heroes of Richard Adams's *Watership Down* (1972) and Ursula K. Le Guin's Earthsea series (1968–2001) are everyday people—or everyday rabbits—saddled with the problems of "country folk." Bilbo and Frodo are hobbits, not hobbit kings.

Martin subverts this, returning instead to a pre-fantasy paradigm. The fourteen major point-of-view characters in A Song of Ice and Fire are not farmers or goatherds; they are men and women of noble birth worried about preserving their station and, in most cases, ruling the world. They have less to do with Le Guin's young wizard Ged than the scheming protagonists of Trollope or Thackeray. And in this way they go against a trend of fiction—genre *and* literary—that has been gaining steam since the Renaissance. Mythic literature concerned kings and demigods, Enlightenment literature focused on nobles, and modern literature brought stories to the street. Martin transports us back to the halls of power, and that's why A Song of Ice and Fire often feels less like a fantasy saga and more like Doris Kearns Goodwin's *Team of Rivals*.

Martin has been praised on Flavorwire by Lev Grossman, fantasy author and fashioner of the "American Tolkien" blurb, for shattering Middle-earth's Manichaeism and replacing it with high-stakes political intrigue. But underlying this is the author's refusal to make his characters naive—another common fantasy trope. "[N]aïveté in fantasy is always a good thing which suggests that the character has retained a willingness to wonder," writes Timmerman. "[T]he pragmatists, the despoiled, the hard-bitten and cynical are often the villains of fantasy."

This is furthest from the truth in A Song of Ice and Fire. Pragmatists are the only survivors of the treachery of Westeros and Essos. The capacity for wonder that enables the childlike protagonists of traditional fantasy to enter another world or to make the best of it is a detriment here. The characters who stay alive are the despoiled—and thus, within Martin's return to high-born Romanticism, we find antiheroes birthed from modern cynics. "[A] hero was too lofty to be utterly defiled, and so he might defile himself," claims the narrator of Dostoyevsky's *Notes from Underground* (1864). More than Frodo or the Pevensie children or even Lovecraft's tormented New Englanders, Tyrion Lannister resembles this modernist icon: what does he spend time on other than defiling himself?

Even the idea of a hero is up for grabs in Martin's work. Fantasy has long been dominated, as has all genre fiction, by the mythic protagonist identified in Joseph Campbell's *The Hero with a Thousand Faces*: the one who leaves home, sacrifices himself for the good of his people, and is reborn to live happily ever after. This figure has become especially boring in film. He is a kid or a cop or a spy, common enough to earn empathy but superhuman enough to avoid the arcs of bullets that kill his companions. We know he's going to win; we just don't know how. That's why Ned Stark's death had such a resonance with the readers of *A Game of Thrones* and the viewers of HBO's retelling. For once, the hero actually bit it—after showing that he was a brave and principled family man against the backdrop of schemers at King's Landing. Showrunners David Benioff and D.B. Weiss, as well as Martin, who served as executive producer, deserve special credit here for ensuring that Ned Stark was the marketing focus of *Game of Thrones*. The poster was Sean Bean on the Iron Throne! Having the guts to chop his head off in episode nine sent a lurch through TV viewers that was comparable to the gasp that greeted Janet Leigh's demise in *Psycho* . . . and that stands as the greatest pop-culture moment of our developing decade.

◆ ◆ ◆

In the course of five books, Martin has lost none of his edge when it comes to killing family men, women, children, babies, and dogs, but he seems to hold a special contempt for the noble heroes who populate traditional fantasy. "*The hero never dies, though. I must be the hero*," wills Quentyn Martell in *A Dance with Dragons*, shortly before he gets roasted. Quentyn's eagerness for glory and deluded self-regard call to mind Don Quixote—and so fantasy comes full circle, poking fun at its past 150 years instead of the centuries of myths that informed Cervantes.

Words are wind, of course, but it's prudent to assume that A Song of Ice and Fire will also violate the most sacred fantasy trope of all: happily ever after. It doesn't look like things will end well for anyone, even Tyrion. "[F]antasy does hold forth as one of its central points the belief that the end of a successful story is joy," claims *Other Worlds*, but the joy in the Seven Kingdoms is more likely to come from a goblet or a girl than any triumph over evil.

Given its impressive subversion of fantasy's most sacred cows, one might expect A Song of Ice and Fire to be the saga that finally pulls fantasy out of the genre ghetto and enables it to be compared side-by-side to, say, Jonathan Franzen's *Freedom* (2010), a similarly hefty meditation on human failure and betrayal. To an extent this has happened; Martin pointed out on his blog that *Time* called *A Dance with Dragons* "the best book of the year (not the best fantasy of the year, or the best SF book of the year, but the Best Book, period)."

But some critics, perhaps frightened by the flatlining sales of literary fiction, have come out even more strongly against genre. As novelist Edward Docx argues in the *Observer*: "[G]enre writers cannot claim to have everything. They can take the money and the sales [. . .]. But they should not be allowed to get away with suggesting that these things tell us anything about the intrinsic value or scope of their work." According to Martin Amis, in a book of essays appropriately titled *The War Against Cliché* (2001), "When we read, we are doing more than delectating words on a page [. . .]. We are communing with the mind of the author." Implicit in his statement is the assumption that genre fiction does not come from unique minds; it comes from common minds that have no aspirations beyond selling to an audience attracted to safe, predictable confines.

It could be argued that George R.R. Martin has quite a unique mind—born in Bayonne, New Jersey, raised in comic book fandom, expert in Lovecraft and Tolkien (as *Dreamsongs* details), tempered by the brutality of Hollywood, and crazy enough about roleplaying games to have a "lost year" devoted to them. But hardcore critics of "science fiction & fantasy" can rightly claim these characteristics as proof that Martin does not escape his roots, that his books are really just souped-up fantasy serials. And worse than the criticism is the condescending praise of literary readers who enjoy slumming in Westeros, such as memoirist Dominique Browning, who praises Martin as an alternative to Tolstoy in a 2012 *New York Times* think piece titled, "Learning to Love Airport Lit."

Some critics have found Martin's writing praiseworthy enough for elevation above the genre fray. The *New York Times* unequivocally anoints him better than Tolkien in its 2011 review of *A Dance with Dragons,* calling his saga "a sprawling and panoramic 19th-century novel turned out in fantasy motley." And Nick Gevers of *Infinity Plus* applauds Martin for his facility with genre itself in a review of Martin's 1982 vampire novel *Fevre Dream*: "[H]is *fin de siècle* canvas may variously take in dying planets, the death of the modern age, or the long decline of chivalry, but loss is always the keynote." These are welcome words, but they do seem to be coming from outside the fantasy genre, from rarefied thinkers impressed with games of a mad world-builder like Lovecraft. Few critics have dared to approach A Song of Ice and Fire from *within* the genre and point out what really makes it so impressive.

Put simply, A Song of Ice and Fire is now vying for a title in fantasy literature that everyone since the scientific romance must have at least conceived of: "Most Complex World." It has hundreds of characters, a daunting and detailed chronology, and, as of this writing, over 4,500 articles on its very own wiki. Those who read it without jumping out of the text to explore the additional material—without immersing themselves in the paratext—miss out on what makes it unique. It's possible to read a sentence like this one, from *A Dance with Dragons*, and dismiss it as a mishmash: "The cobbler told them how the body of the Butcher King had been disinterred and clad in copper armor, after the Green Grace of Astapor had a vision that he would deliver them from the Yunkai'i." But the four proper names in there, requiring four trips to the map or appendix if you haven't been paying attention, make A Song of Ice and Fire require close reading just as much as any modernist literary masterwork, albeit of a different, nerdier stripe.

Martin thus fights the genre wars by sidestepping them. Working from within the system, refusing to apologize for what came before, he writes books that are too bloody, unexpected, and relentlessly story-driven to be ignored. In doing so, he elevates other fantasy along with his own. Praise from respected outlets like The *New York Times* doesn't just help A Song of Ice and Fire, it legitimizes the fantasy that came before—works, for example, by Peter S. Beagle, Roger Zelazny, and Michael Moorcock—while making the world safe for literary novelists like Lev Grossman to try their hand at fantasy, in Grossman's case with the successful Magicians series.

It's unlikely that the "fantasy & science fiction" section of your local bookstore will disappear anytime soon (well, until the bookstore does), or that fantasy books will begin appearing on the front page of the *New York Times Book Review* along with tales of twenty-first-century anomie. Some hardcore academic critics will always stick to their guns and discount any novel that isn't strictly realist as "a boy's game," perhaps more viciously than ever as the real boy's games threaten to prevent the next generation from reading at all.

But in the genre wars, Martin is sitting pretty. His twisting of expectations has silenced some genre-haters and won over the culture mavens—and his industrious pacifism honors his genre roots. He's like Bill Hicks's pot smokers sitting in trees during the War on Drugs: "Are they fighting us? We're not even in that fucking field!" It's a brilliant strategy worthy of his characters.

◆ ◆ ◆

Since Stevenson, responding to Henry James, genre writers have been on the defensive, trying to stick up for their work as if there were something wrong with it to begin with. In a 2007 interview on Pat's Fantasy Hotlist, Martin declared: "None of us wants to be consigned to the playpen, or have our work dismissed as unworthy of serious consideration as literature because of the label on the spine. Myself, I think a story is a story is a story, and the only thing worth writing about is the human heart in conflict with itself."

That would seem like a statement all critics can get behind, genre and literary alike. For my own foray into fantasy, I don't need a blurb from George R.R. Martin to approve of what I'm doing. He's lifted all the boats with A Song of Ice and Fire, making it okay for people like me—and those with much more literary credibility—to get in touch with our inner fantasy lover, while at the same time challenging us to do better with the quality of his work.

◆ ◆ ◆

NED VIZZINI is the author of *It's Kind of a Funny Story*, *Be More Chill*, and *Teen Angst? Naaah. . . .* He has written for The *New York Times*, The Daily Beast, and MTV's *Teen Wolf*. His work has been translated into seven languages. He is the co-author, with Chris Columbus, of the forthcoming fantasy-adventure series House of Secrets. He has contributed to Smart Pop anthologies about The Hunger Games, The Chronicles of Narnia, and *The Walking Dead*. He has spoken at over two hundred universities, libraries, and schools around the world about writing and mental health. He received an award from UCLA in 2011 for Excellence in Public Advocacy Through the Arts. Ned lives in Los Angeles with his wife, Sabra Embury, and their son. His next novel, *The Other Normals*, will be published by HarperCollins on September 25, 2012.

ACKNOWLEDGMENTS

THANKS TO Glenn Yeffeth, publisher and CEO of BenBella Books, for once again allowing me the chance to add to the Smart Pop imprint; Heather Butterfield for enthusiastic and inventive marketing support; Leigh Camp for production magic; the crack team of copyeditors and designers who made all of us look better; and most especially Leah Wilson, Smart Pop editor-in-chief, who, through her own high standards and tireless efforts on behalf of the line, inspires me to always push myself harder, yet manages somehow to keep the often-daunting anthology editing process a lot more fun than it has any right to be. Beyond the BenBella offices in Texas and Massachusetts, support and suggestions for the book were also provided by James John Bell, Scott Cuthberston, Stephen Dedman, Marc Fishman, Jeremy Jones, Helen Merrick, Chris Pramas, Jeff VanderMeer, and Stewart Woods.

The best part of any anthology for me is getting to collaborate with so many writers whose work I enjoy and admire. *Beyond the Wall* boasts contributions from a lineup of essayists possessing good humor, professionalism, and talent—everything an editor could ask for. Thanks to their agents, for helping to make their participation possible. And special thanks to R.A. Salvatore. From conversations about fantasy fiction Bob and I have had—and there have been many since he contributed a short story to the first anthology I edited, way back in 1993—I knew that he was a great choice to open the collection. I'm glad he agreed.

Finally, my participation in *Beyond the Wall*—in fact the book itself—would not have been possible without George R.R. Martin. In addition to giving us all something spectacular to talk about with A Song of Ice and Fire, George, along with his tireless assistant Ty Franck, helped me to get the project rolling at the 2011 San Diego Comic-Con and pointed me toward several of the key essayists. His graciousness and generosity is matched only by his vision and skill as an author.

ABOUT THE EDITOR

JAMES LOWDER has edited book lines or series for both large and small houses and has helmed such critically acclaimed anthologies as *Curse of the Full Moon*, *The Doom of Camelot*, the Books of Flesh trilogy, and the 2011 Smart Pop release *Triumph of The Walking Dead*. As an author, his publications include the bestselling, widely translated dark fantasy novels *Prince of Lies* and *Knight of the Black Rose*, short fiction for such anthologies as *Shadows over Baker Street* and *The Repentant*, and comic book scripts for Image, Moonstone, and DC. He's written hundreds of feature articles, essays, film reviews, and book reviews for publications ranging from *Amazing Stories* and *The New England Journal of History* to BenBella's *King Kong is Back!* and *The Unauthorized X-Men*. His work has received five Origins Awards and an ENnie Award, and been nominated for the International Horror Guild Award and the Bram Stoker Award. Online at jameslowder.com.